The Fourth
of July Wake

The Fourth of July Wake

Harold Adams

Five Star • Waterville, Maine

This novel is a work of fiction. Names, characters, places and incidents are either the product of the author's imagination, or, if real, used fictitiously.

First Edition, Second Printing

Published in 2003 in conjunction with Tekno Books and Ed Gorman.

Set in 11 pt. Plantin by Myrna S. Raven.

Printed in the United States on permanent paper.

Library of Congress Cataloging-in-Publication Data

Adams, Harold, 1923–
    The Fourth of July wake / Harold Adams.
       p. cm.—(Five Star first edition mystery series)
    ISBN 0-7862-3000-2 (hc : alk. paper)
    1. Middle West—Fiction.   2. Wake services—Fiction.
  3. Inheritance and succession—Fiction. I. Title. II. Series.
  PS3551.D367 F59
   813'.54—dc21   2002192850

This book is dedicated to Barbara Mayor,
in-house editor through my
entire publishing career.
I am also indebted to Ivy Fisher Stone,
who has been an ideal agent and
a close friend for two decades.

Chapter 1

"How'd you like to attend a wake?" Matt asked.

I propped the telephone between the pillow and my ear and asked, "Whose?"

"P.J.'s. His widow, Sorah, is throwing a discreet wingding in his honor, which she says is what he wanted."

I wondered how I could be dreaming when I hadn't been asleep. P.J. was Matt Krueger's father, who, the last I knew, was in his late sixties and king of all he surveyed and some beyond, with the exception of his robustly ageless wife, Elizabeth, who was absolute ruler on the home front.

"Who's Sorah?" I asked.

"The new wife he married a year and a half ago. She's about twenty-four, which makes her only forty years his junior. I guess you and I've been out of touch longer than I realized."

Matt and I had shared freshman classes at the University of Minnesota several years back, and I'd visited his cabin each summer during college and a few times after graduation until he began teaching somewhere out west.

"Tell me about Sorah," I said.

"It'd take a while and you might not believe me. Better you should see her in the flesh, and even then you might not believe. She used to call P.J. 'Daddy,' but don't jump to conclusions until you meet her. Maybe not then."

"Okay. What's Marcia think of her?"

Marcia was his aristocratic sister-in-law who'd been second in command to Elizabeth and the family's enforcer of proper clan conduct back when I visited at the lake.

Matt sighed. "She thinks Sorah murdered P.J. I guess I'd better tell you; one reason I'm asking you into this mess is because she pushed me to."

"Why?"

"I made the mistake of telling her you solved the Fletcher murder down in Mexico."

"How'd P.J. die?"

"His heart crapped out. Why? Nobody's said so I could understand. I told Marcia if it was romancing a wife who was younger than his daughter, nobody's going to consider it anything but a lovely way of suicide."

"What makes Marcia so bitter?"

"Oh, nothing really special—except P.J. made Sorah his sole heir. None of the family gets a dime. It was no surprise. He told me a while back that none of us needed any help from him, and that was hard to argue."

He went on to explain the gathering wasn't really a wake. P.J. died nearly three months ago after willing his body to the University of Minnesota Hospital for research and leaving orders that there should be no funeral. Sorah decided to hold a memorial family gathering, and since all of them went to the lake during the Fourth of July she figured that was the appropriate time and place.

He went on to assure me he really wanted us to get together again and said I was welcome to bring along a friend. Since the Fourth fell on Monday, he suggested I come around the Thursday before and case the situation in advance.

I said my latest romance had folded so I'd be coming alone.

"Great, maybe we can line you up with someone."

The drive to Bent Pine Lake from Minneapolis takes a

8

little under three hours and I spent most of that time trying to assess Matt's attitude about his father's death. P.J. had never been the pal-type father, but he wasn't a martinet or totally remote, and back when I was close to the family, I'd always felt there was something approaching reverence toward him by his offspring. No doubt the old man's marriage to a woman young enough to be his granddaughter had shattered a few illusions and raised some hackles, but I sensed Matt was remarkably untouched by the death and that seemed uncharacteristic of the man I remembered.

It was half past seven when I turned off the country highway and approached Matt's cabin. The rutted road ran through a forest of jack pines, soft maples and scrub brush and ended in a small parking area immediately behind the back porch. A high, boxy four-wheel drive pickup squatted near the rear door, looking as if it'd jump if you whistled. I was surprised no one else had arrived yet, until I recalled Fridays were when the crowds gathered at the lake.

I had a moment's disorientation at first sight of the cabin before realizing that since my last visit, he'd added a wing, doubling its size.

When I got out and slammed my car door, Matt appeared, grinning, He'd grown a goatee and mustache since our last meeting, but the warm smile, high forehead and mischievous eyes were unmistakable.

We exchanged the usual greetings of old classmates and he led me into the original wing through the rear door on an enclosed porch, past the kitchen and into the living room.

Marcia was seated on a couch facing the fireplace, which occupied the center of the room. She had always reminded me of a Siamese cat, which was ridiculous because her eyes were brown, not blue, and her hair was almost black. The impression came from her sleek, aristocratic bearing and the cold, judgmental eyes. Now her face was fuller and her upper body seemed larger while her hips and legs were slim as before. Her skin was smooth and glowing. She wore black slacks and a white sweater with large black splashes in no apparent pattern. I accepted her cool hand and returned her polite smile while remembering her condescension toward me in the past.

I asked where her husband Luke was.

"Playing poker in our cabin," she said.

Luke was Matt's younger brother and CEO of the advertising firm, Krueger, Callahan and Commers. He was by far the most financially successful of P.J.'s descendents.

She asked what I'd been doing since my return from Mexico and didn't listen to my answer. When she felt the social obligations had been met, she got down to business.

"I assume Matt's told you why I wanted you here this weekend?"

"He hinted it was an in-law problem," I said.

"She thinks it's an out-law one," said Matt.

She gave him a disapproving frown and informed us both that this was anything but a frivolous matter. "I won't believe P.J.'s death was natural, and I'd like to explain my reasons to Kyle without a lot of kidding around."

"You want me to go play poker with the guys?" he asked.

"That's a lovely idea."

He tried to hide his annoyance with a smile, said he'd see me later, and left.

Marcia suggested I make a drink for myself if I was so inclined. I was, and offered to mix something for her.

"Sherry, please."

After serving her I mixed a gin and tonic for me, settled into a sagging chair by the fireplace and waited.

She started speaking with quiet deliberation. "I must ask

you to be very objective and professional about what I have to say. I'll be critical of Matt, but you must understand what's involved here. He refuses to look at reality in all this because he's the one who brought Sorah here in the first place, introduced her to his father, and can't escape at least part of the responsibility for what has happened. The truth is, like most men, he's been besotted by that woman since the moment he first saw her."

She halted a moment, apparently realizing she had let her bitterness show too deeply, and took a sip of her sherry. When she spoke again she had recovered her objective tone.

"I suppose that you know Elizabeth died four years ago?"

"No. Matt gave me no details."

I hadn't quite managed to accept the fact that the chubby, aggressive and strong-minded queen of the Krueger clan could die. She had seemed indomitable, the only person in their world not overwhelmed by her husband's personality. She'd always felt he failed to appreciate their children and openly mocked his inflated ego, tireless ambition, and constant pursuit of public recognition. Her put-downs had been classic and frequent, but he always seemed impervious.

Marcia told me Elizabeth died of cancer six months after it was diagnosed. I felt a wave of depression, which must have shown. Marcia frowned impatiently and leaned forward.

"P.J. handled the loss magnificently, never broke down, not even at the funeral—which he hated. All right. Sorah went for P.J. the moment she saw his house and car. Did you know he bought a Mercedes after Elizabeth died? Just two months after. A sports model. Like something professional athletes and rock stars think they have to own. Sorah saw it and immediately told P.J. she thought there was nothing more interesting than mature men with young ideas."

She sipped her sherry and stared into the empty fireplace.

"I wasn't worried then. Thought he was too smart to be taken in by such a tart, and on top of that I knew he wasn't capable of, well, let me be blunt—he was impotent."

I wondered how she would know that and she smiled.

"How'd I know? Elizabeth told me. She was glad because she didn't have to worry about him womanizing any more. He'd been, to put it politely, vulnerable to younger women from the time he was forty-five—probably even earlier. Like most men."

"Maybe the girl wanted a father, not a lover."

She shook her head in wonder.

"You were always naive, Kyle, but in your new field of expertise that could be fatal. Matt has never picked a woman who wasn't, shall we say, sexually precocious or at least promising. Sorah was smart enough to play hard to get, and he pretends he never got anywhere, but I won't swallow that. I think his claim that she was a charming waif looking for a father is specious, and I've told him so."

"What do you want to prove?"

"I want it proved that she killed him. She was a nurse, you know. She'd know just how to go about it. Somehow she convinced P.J. he could be a perpetual lover, and married him for his money, and once she had him wrapped up, got rid of him. I want that proved. I'm willing to pay for it."

I didn't have to ask if husband Luke was willing. He was not, I knew from the past, about to knock heads with Marcia.

"I doubt I can do much with this one," I said.

"I'm not asking you to plunge in. Just stay with us through this long weekend, watch what goes on, keep your eyes open. You'll see I'm right. You've a quick eye and a sharp wit. I noticed that long ago, and I know from your background you hate a fraud. You'll soon see I'm right."

My agreement to give it a try brought on her magnificent smile, which had a lot to do with her success in getting her way. This time, when she asked what I was doing about my future, she managed to look interested for several seconds before she slipped in gently during a pause in my monologue and assured me I'd do just fine. Then she finished her sherry, thanked me warmly for coming, said she hoped I'd have a lovely time, and wished me good-night.

I found a *Rumpole of the Bailey Omnibus* in Matt's library of paperbacks and read until near midnight, when I put it down, went outside, walked down to the dock and stared across the calm, dark lake. As I headed up toward the cabin, I noticed a new high-back bench a couple steps off the path, and sat down on it. The only sounds were croaking bullfrogs that pulsed away in steady rhythm. There wasn't a light in view across the lake. A falling star hurtled across the northeastern sky too fast to follow, but when I turned my head I spotted movement a few yards to my right.

He was no more than a shift in the shadows when I first sensed him. The night was moonless, the Milky Way sparkled white across the black sky reflecting faintly on the water before me. I watched the movement from the corner of my eye and made out a man staring at the cabin a dozen yards up and away from the shore as he moved silently, half crouched, almost hunchbacked, with hands dangling apishly near his knees.

About three yards short of me, he glanced at the path before him, caught sight of me in the night and went rigid. Then he was gone. I was sure he'd darted into the woods to my right, but it seemed he had simply dissipated. Except for the initial scraping and one snapped twig, there wasn't a thing to tell me he existed.

I stood, took a step forward and listened. Either he moved like a ghost or had frozen in the shadows. His awful secretiveness made me reject trying to follow him.

After a moment I walked as casually as I could up the rude path to the cabin.

Chapter 2

I slept in the lower bunk of what Matt called Cell #1 in a row of three rooms lining the new east wing. It was large enough for upper and lower bunks, a bureau, a footlocker and one straight-backed chair. A heavy curtain slid across the doorway, offering at least partial privacy.

Normally I sleep best through dawn, but that morning I was up with the sun. After bathroom routines I dressed, walked into the old wing and found Matt in the tiny kitchen mixing pancake batter with fresh blueberries picked from his front yard.

"You're just in time to pour orange juice," he told me. "Did Marcia convince you of anything last night?"

"I'm pretty sure she doesn't much like her mother-in-law."

He laughed, poured batter into the griddle and shook his head.

"Marcia's real problem is having a mother-in-law young enough to be her daughter. It gnaws on her. On top of that, after Elizabeth died, Marcia was P.J.'s family prime minister, boss of the realm. Then Sorah came and phtt! To make it worse, Marcia couldn't hide her jealousy and P.J. froze her out. As you might guess, Marcia couldn't believe Sorah hadn't made a project of that, so naturally it follows, Sorah must've murdered P.J. Two and two make eight, right?"

"For her, I guess so."

"In addition, Marcia has diabetes. It came on about three years ago and she thinks it makes her less royal.

That's part of why she was vulnerable to Sorah's campaign."

We ate breakfast at a small table by corner windows in the new living room and caught glimpses of a jewel-bright, green hummingbird at a feeder a few feet outside.

I turned back to Matt and asked how his brother Luke felt about the new widow.

"He's got a problem. Sorah's a charmer and he can't help liking her, but at the same time he's convinced Marcia's always right, so he can't just shrug off her murder obsession."

"How about sister Peg and her husband, Burt?"

"Peg doesn't believe anybody's really bad. She liked Sorah from the start, even thought she was good for P.J. Burt? Who knows? He's into raising money for charity, so anybody with lots to give can't be all bad."

I remembered vaguely how disappointed Matt had been when Peg married Burt, but then, as now, he was not inclined to elaborate on his prejudices.

I went into the kitchen for the coffee pot, refilled our cups, sat down and watched him until he met my eyes.

"How close were you and Sorah before she married your dad?"

His smile took some effort.

"I never slept with her, if that's your question. She came here with friends, stayed overnight a couple times when there was lots of company. I'd have liked it otherwise, naturally. Even kissed her a couple times. She's affectionate and seemed to like it, but that was the limit. How about we go fishing?"

That sounded good to me so he got fishing rods for both of us and his kit of baits and hooks, and we headed down to the beach.

He rowed us away from the dock and out around the peninsula which gave the lake a modified horseshoe shape, and dropped anchor in the narrow western bay near a patch of water lilies lining the shore.

I still-fished for blue gills while he cast toward shore among the pads, trying for bass. I caught three blue gills in a row, one too small to keep, before he hooked a bass. When nothing happened after that flurry, we moved farther west and then some south. Sniffles, as Matt said.

Around ten we headed back to the eastern shore and docked below P.J.'s white cabin. It stood on a knoll, and its giant bay window with multiple panes two stories high dominated the lake like a castle on an island.

"Sorah likes fish for breakfast," said Matt. "She ought to be about ready for these by now."

We tied up the boat and climbed the long path to the front porch. Estelle, P.J.'s anonymous-faced housekeeper with the eye-catching body, greeted us, took the fish and said Sorah would be down directly. We wandered into the two-story living room with its monstrous stone fireplace and balcony along the back. I knew from visits in the past that there were four bedrooms up there, each with a private bath.

We parked on leather upholstered chairs and Matt thumbed a *Vogue* magazine taken from a vast, glass-topped coffee table.

A voice from above called "Hi!" and I looked up at a face with a movie star complexion, wide eyes, high cheeks, a nose almost too long and a ripe mouth. Mahogany brown hair, cut short, softly framed her features.

"Estelle says you brought fresh fish for breakfast—I hope you haven't eaten?"

Her voice was low-pitched, almost husky.

"We didn't catch enough to earn a meal," Matt told her. "They're all for you. This is an old college buddy of mine, Kyle Champion."

She descended the stairs like an actress making an entrance but with a smile that mocked her show.

"I remember seeing you on TV," she said, warmly clasping my hand with both of hers. "You look taller in person."

"Something about being in front of those cameras shrinks a man," I said.

"Well, we're all proud you could come for the memorial party. That's what I call it. P.J. once told me he'd only tolerate a wake, but I know he was kidding. Can I offer you anything?"

"Coffee'd be great," Matt assured her. A few moments later we were in a bright kitchen sitting in a booth across from her and drinking coffee, while fish sizzled in the frying pan across the room under Estelle's watchful eyes.

"We're going to have a barbecue at the pit out front," Sorah told me. "All the family will be there. We could have had hundreds of guests, but I know P.J. preferred intimate groups, so I've asked only a few very close business friends in addition to the family." She smiled at Matt. "I even persuaded Jerry to come with Phyl. It may cause some problems since he and Marcia are strictly like cat and dog, but I hope you'll help me keep matters in hand."

She turned back to me. "Did you know that P.J. often watched your show back when you anchored the news? He remembered you visiting here at the lake."

"He was quite a guy," I said. "I admired him."

"Everybody did."

She said that with flat assurance and suddenly rose to join Estelle at the stove across the room. I wasn't certain whether it was because she was going to cry or wanted me to think she might. Matt looked at her with an expression I couldn't read.

"How long were they married?" I asked him quietly.

He looked at me, as if my presence were a surprise, then said it had been eighteen months.

"They live here all that time?"

"No. They honeymooned in England about two months. I told Luke it was probably to give Marcia a chance to recover from the shock, but more likely it was to impress Sorah. You can't believe how hard P.J. worked at that. He claimed it was a matter of educating her, but that was malarkey. He never got over having a woman that young and beautiful crazy about him. P.J. didn't brag with his mouth, he demonstrated. Taking her to England let her see the class of people he'd been important to back when he was doing a lot of business there. The people he introduced her to could do his bragging for him."

Sorah came back to join us accompanied by Estelle, who carried two of the blue gills on a plate with bacon and toast and set them before her as she took her chair. After refilling our coffee cups, Estelle moved off.

Matt looked at Sorah whose face was sober and thoughtful as she began eating.

"Somehow," said Matt, "this reminds me of the last time Sorah was staying at my place with friends. I was making *coq au vin* and cooking up a storm, and I said, 'When men cook, they're good cooks.' And she said, 'When men talk, they brag.' I guess that's one of the reasons P.J. impressed her. He never bragged."

"I knew you were only kidding," Sorah said earnestly. "I was just kidding back."

He said of course she was and drank his coffee.

I couldn't decide what their relationship was. It wasn't mother-in-law to son-in-law or even slight sibling, nor did it seem sexual.

Sorah ate with concentration, and at first I thought she paid no attention when Matt asked questions about my trip to France the previous summer. But when he made reference to murder on the barge, her eyes lifted to take me in with more interest than she'd shown while greeting me as a minor celebrity.

After Estelle cleared away the dishes, Sorah rested her elbows on the table and cupped her chin.

"You were involved with another murder, weren't you? In Mexico?"

I admitted I was.

"How interesting. I don't suppose your involvement with things like that has anything at all to do with your coming here this weekend?"

"Of course not—" began Matt.

"Let him answer," said Sorah, smiling gently.

"I knew P.J.," I reminded her.

"Hundreds of people knew him. But I believe you're the only person not related, at least by marriage, who's been invited by any member of the family but me. Did you know that?"

"No."

She looked at Matt. "Marcia asked you to invite him, didn't she?"

"He's an old friend to all of us," said Matt, looking miserable.

Sorah laughed and reached over to put her slim hand on mine.

"It's okay, Kyle, I'm glad you're here, for whatever reason, and you're welcome. But please, don't think I'm

20

stupid. Just do your thing and have fun."

When we left the kitchen a few moments later, I glanced at Estelle in passing and met a flat, enigmatic stare that made me think she had missed nothing but gave no hint as to what it meant to her.

Sorah saw us out, and as we walked down to the boat I asked Matt what Estelle's attitude had been toward P.J.'s marriage.

"A good question," he said. "I'd lay odds nobody in the family could tell you. My personal notion is, if P.J. accepted her, Estelle did and will stand by her. I don't think anybody could convince Estelle that P.J.'d let any kid make a fool of him. And you can be sure Sorah treats her right to keep on her good side. She's smart enough to know the woman's priceless."

Chapter 3

After returning to Matt's dock and securing the boat, we walked up the path until I stopped him by the bench and described what I'd seen from there the night before. He wanted to know exactly where the ghost had disappeared and poked about in the brush looking for signs of an intruder. The ground was littered with pine needles, and while there were vague indentations in the sandy soil, neither of us could find identifiable footprints.

"We need an old-time tracker," he complained.

"Could the guy have been one of your neighbors?" I asked.

"It sounds like something old Thorvald might do. He had a farm north of the lake, but they put him away about three or four years ago. I can't believe he's been let out."

"Why was he put away?"

"Well, he's what they used to call nuts and now say is mentally disturbed. He sure as hell disturbed the locals. It started with him chasing kids off his property with more enthusiasm than the parents appreciated. Then he clobbered P.J.'s dog Patsy with an axe because she'd been worrying his chickens. The district attorney made him pay for the pooch and thought that'd settle him down."

"Then what?"

"Then the old bastard fired warning shots at a couple deer hunters. One of them claimed he felt the slug graze his hat brim."

"He have any reason to be sore at you?"

"Not personally. Of course, he was sore at P.J. over

having to pay for the dog, and he might've held that against the whole family. I suppose I'd better check and see if he's still locked up."

That was postponed because the closest phone was at Sorah's house. Matt's only concession to technology in the cabin was a hi-fi radio-phonograph combination which was totally obsolete. He still owned and played honest-to-God records. His set wouldn't take CDs or cassettes and he had no television.

I was in the bathroom when a car pulled up in back of the cabin. Matt greeted someone enthusiastically but I heard no response. When I entered the old wing, a man stood just inside the door, facing Matt. His bulk shrank the kitchen. He must have ducked his head to enter the door and probably had to turn sidewise coming through it. His slab jaw would make George Washington look weak-chinned; his neck was wider than the top of his blond head. As he glanced over Matt with bloodshot, weary eyes, I guessed he was a drunk.

Matt introduced him as Handy Anderson, an old lifeguard partner from a lifetime back.

"You can guess who all the girls fell for," said Matt, "but he was so shy he hardly spoke to them."

"Pleasure," said Handy. His voice was almost a whisper, as though squeezed off by all the muscle. When his hand engulfed mine, I winced, expecting crushed fingers, but his grip was gentle despite a palm hard and rough as oak.

"You look bushed," said Matt. "How long have you been driving?"

"About twenty-four hours," he whispered. "Hey, I hope I'm not butting in on anything—?"

"I never do anything with guys that'd keep me from welcoming old friends. Kyle and I were at the U. together. He's

23

been in the TV business, but don't hold that against him. How about lunch? You look like you need something."

"Don't want to be a bother, but I—" he broke off, took a deep breath and released it in a long sigh. "I got this girl, Ann Rose, out in the car and—"

"Well for God's sake, bring her in!"

Handy looked at me with an expression of terrible embarrassment.

"We're not married yet—been driving all night—she's dead asleep in the back of my car—"

"So carry her in and put her in a bunk," said Matt. "Go on, for God's sake, get her comfortable."

He protested that she might be embarrassed, and Matt said don't be silly. Finally the giant turned and went through the door with the slouching grace of a lion.

"She must be a shrinking violet," I said.

Matt grinned and shook his head. "He wants to think all women are. Despite all the years they've been trying to rape him, Handy just won't believe anything else."

"Is he drunk?"

"Lord no, just punchy from the long drive. He never touches meat, alcohol or drugs."

We both looked out and watched the giant walk back from his whopping SUV, carrying what in his huge arms looked like a child. She was wrapped in a plaid blanket that hid her face. Matt led him into the new wing and had him park her in the room immediately adjacent to the toilet. We heard a low murmur and a moment later Handy came out, carefully drew the curtain, and followed us back to the kitchen.

He turned down pancakes or even vegetable soup but settled for two oranges, a grapefruit, and half a loaf of toasted wheat bread. It was all consumed with a reverent air, as if he were taking communion, only making a complete banquet out of it.

Later he told us they'd come from southern Iowa where Ann Rose's parents lived. She'd had an argument with her mother and decided to leave home. Wanted to get married. They got a license in St. Cloud but learned there was a waiting period and after some discussion agreed they should come to Matt's place and get the actual wedding taken care of later.

"You got a sleeping bag I can use on the back porch?" he asked.

"Friend, you obviously haven't looked around this place any. There's nobody here but Kyle and me, and there are bunks galore. If you insist on purity you can use the room between Kyle and Ann Rose."

He accepted that and a few minutes later was sacked out. Matt took my arm and led me out through the front door.

"We'll just leave them," he said. "Marcia's expecting us for lunch. We might as well drop by now."

Matt's cabin was the only one in the Krueger row where trees hadn't been cleared to give an unbroken view of the lake. Matt liked the water seen through the trees and besides that, hated lawn mowers, leaf blowers and chain saws, all abominations that made ghastly noise.

We walked across P.J.'s broad grounds through a short stretch of young Norway pine, and came in view of Marcia and Luke's posh log cabin tucked into the curving slope that ran down to the shore which arched north at that point.

The old man's place had been built to give and provide a view. Luke's place simply blended in. The logs were painted a flat, pale green that camouflaged the place in summer. We went up a neat path trimmed with half-sunken logs and occasional flower boxes filled with red and white blossoms. An eight-year-old brunette in a green tank suit regarded us with large brown eyes under a high forehead, smiled at Matt and gave me a quick, shy glance when he introduced her as Sandra.

"Don't call her Sandy," he warned.

Inside I met her four-year-old brother Billy, who was equally dark haired, brown-eyed and shy.

Marcia came out of the kitchen wearing a brief cover-up over a red and white flowered one-piece swimming suit. Her legs were beautiful as ever with fine thighs tapering to smooth knees, trim calves and aristocratic ankles.

She said lunch was about ready and asked what we'd like to drink. We agreed on beer.

She served us in an alcove off the front living room at a table for eight, but only four of us shared it. The children had already been fed and went out to the beach as we sat down. All the Krueger family made a point of teaching their offspring to swim from next to infancy, so no one worried about them falling off the dock.

Luke came in from the backyard where he'd been replacing the spark plug in his lawn mower. His hairless body was bronzed, flat bellied, and while the waist had thickened a little, his shoulders were broad enough to keep him looking fit as ever. I noticed the hairline had begun a modest retreat.

He gave me his tight grin and a strong hand, which I met hard knowing he liked to apply pressure. He laughed, told me I was looking good and took a drink from his beer mug as he settled at the table head.

"What'd you think of Sorah?" Marcia asked, passing a stack of assorted sandwiches.

"Very attractive," I said, choosing what looked and smelled like pastrami.

Marcia turned to Matt. "Did she go after him?"

"You'd probably think so. Said she'd seen him on TV and while she didn't exactly rave, she let him know P.J. was fond of his show."

"Typical," said Marcia. She made the word sound sympathetic, as if Sorah were more to be pitied than censured.

"And very soon she let us both know that she'd figured out why he's here and that she wasn't worried."

Marcia gave him an exasperated look. "Matt, you said something to warn her, didn't you? Started telling her about Kyle's detective work . . ."

"Well, we were just talking and it was natural to give her some background . . ."

"Oh, of course. All right. And she took it all in with her usual gracious, condescending smile. Right?"

"She wasn't condescending at all. Took it very well, actually."

"Ah, what a sly minx!"

A little later she asked how I planned to begin my investigation and I admitted I hadn't the foggiest notion. That answer didn't please her any more than it did me.

Talk moved on to the sighting of Thorvald, which reminded Matt he was going to check with authorities about his status and went to use Luke's telephone. While he was at it, Sandra ran in and announced there was a big dead fish without any head on the dock. I walked with Luke to see.

It was a big northern, about ten pounds, laid neatly dead center in the last section of the dock. Its scales had faded to gray in the hot sun and flies buzzed and swarmed where the head had been chopped off.

Luke scowled, turned to the live bait box attached to the

dock side and raised the hinged lid. I knew the Kruegers often put catches in it when they hadn't hooked enough for a meal and saved them for a day or so.

"What's the deal?" I asked.

Luke shrugged and told Sandra to carry the fish to the upper beach, bury it, and take Billy along to help. Neither of them liked the order, but they did as they were told promptly.

"I don't get it," said Luke, scowling. "I caught that one yesterday late and put him in the box. Why'd somebody net him, chop his head off and leave him out here?"

"Think it could have been Thorvald?" I asked.

He stared at me, then looked toward the cabin as Matt came out the front door and headed for us.

"What's wrong?" he asked when he saw Luke's expression.

Luke told him.

"Weird," said Matt, "but I'm afraid it couldn't have been Thorvald. When I called the authorities they told me he was killed in a bus accident on Old Shakopee Road about five months ago."

"Well then," said Luke, shrugging, "it must have been some punks messing around."

He didn't sound convinced of that.

"Yeah," agreed Matt. "I think you better keep a close eye on the kids for a while, huh?"

When the two children came back to join us, Luke sent them to tell their mother what they'd done. They took off.

The three of us sat dangling our legs over the dockside and stared at a lone fisherman casting lazily from a rowboat out in the bay. Luke said the damned fool'd never catch anything there.

I asked how he felt about Marcia hiring me.

The question brought a pained look followed by a frown and shrug.

"She's always got to do her thing."

"You think she's right?"

He stared at the fisherman casting in the bay.

"I can't believe Sorah would kill P.J. Just can't. But then, I couldn't believe Clinton could win a second term, so what the hell do I know?"

"Did Marcia have Clinton's win figured?"

"Oh yeah. She's all Republican and has a way of intuiting party disasters. Makes it hard to ignore her feelings now."

"Have you talked about this business with Peg and Burt?" I asked.

"No. They haven't been up to the lake in the last couple weeks. We expect them Friday."

"How'd Peg feel about Sorah?"

"Oh, she was shook up at first, but you know her. She likes everybody and accepted Sorah quicker than any of the rest of us. Right away she worried about her feeling like an outsider, especially when Marcia's played the snotty bitch."

"How'd Burt feel?"

"Embarrassed. Just like when P.J. bought the sports car. He figured the money should have gone to a cancer research fund or maybe the symphony orchestra. You can imagine the kind of ribbing he took from his buddies in the business about missing out on his father-in-law's bundle."

Burt was currently fundraising for the University Foundation. Back when I'd been a news researcher for TV, I'd done a charities fraud report that rattled him thoroughly. He came to see me with a couple of cohorts and said such reportage smeared all charities with the same slime brush. The sibilance of that line remained etched in my mind.

We walked back up to the cabin, and Marcia asked what was going on. When she'd heard everything, she said Luke should call the police.

He tried to smile but couldn't conceal his impatience.

"What'll I report? An attack on a dead fish? The sighting of a ghost by a guest?"

She wasn't amused and, as her face turned red, Matt edged me toward the door and said we had to leave. I could hear her voice, low and angry as we went down the path.

Back in the old wing of Matt's place, I asked him for a list of people Sorah had come to the cabin with. He said there were only two: his brother, Jerry, and a girlfriend named Phyllis.

"Jerry? My God, I'd forgotten him. What is he now, about twenty-some?"

"Twenty-six. He's the only one of us without a cabin up here. He ran away, you know, when he was just fourteen. P.J. never let him come back. It was a hell of a time. Jerry got into lots of trouble. Now he writes poetry, mostly scatological, and a little serious fiction, which he can't sell but he gets into little mags now and then. Makes his living selling pornography. As he puts it, he's erratically erotic. Produces about four of what he calls 'uck' novels in as many months, then burns out and tries other things until he needs money again."

"What's Phyllis do?"

"She's a nurse at a clinic near downtown Minneapolis."

"Can you give me a telephone number for each of them?"

He could and did. I didn't want to be talking to people from a telephone where anyone could overhear, so he took me to his sister's place, which was vacant for the day, and set me up with her phone and a notepad.

Jerry answered the way writers who are having trouble always do: on the first ring, eager for escape.

I gave him my name and told him where I was calling from.

He placed me at once and expressed some surprise that I'd be calling from Kruegerland. "I assumed you'd gone far beyond all that."

"I'm trying to get some information about Sorah."

"Ah, the game's afoot, right? Or in this case, patricide, I assume."

"How'd you meet Sorah?"

"She worked in the same clinic with Phyl. They coffeed together, lunched, talked about work. Great buddies."

"What'd they do in this clinic—was it a general deal—?"

"Plumbing. All the stuff to do with urinary channels and depressing matters related thereto."

"Including potency problems?"

"You got it nailed, Pal. The big deal, and I say that advisedly since that's one of the tragedies of man, implicitly. I don't know the medical term but you follow, I trust?"

I thought I did.

"Could I talk with Phyllis?" I asked.

He said she'd be home around four, and after checking with Matt, I asked him to have her call us collect and gave him Burt's number. He agreed.

Matt and I killed the two-hour wait playing badminton on a beach court where the sand was soft and a small pine tree inside one edge of the court was an automatic out-of-bounds if you hit it or fell into it. Fast footwork was out of the question, and there was an occasionally honored gentlemen's agreement that you didn't knock the bird more than a yard out of center court. Matt won two out of three games, which I considered a moral victory for me since he played in that stupid court regularly and should have murdered me.

I refused to concede that he'd have done better if he hadn't been laughing so hard at my efforts on that lousy court.

We went for a swim after getting sweated up and were in the cabin drinking cold Leinenkugel beer when Phyl's call came. Matt answered in case it was a family call, and I gathered from his end of the dialogue that Phyllis was mad at the notion anyone would even suspect Sorah of doing anything remotely evil, least of all murder. Matt managed to cool her down a little before handing me the phone.

She started off calling me Mister Champion and went on to say much of what I guessed Matt had already heard. She concluded it was unlikely there was anything I could learn from her that would be anything but supportive of Sorah and, in case I didn't know, she heartily despised Marcia. "So why ask?"

I assured her I'd met Sorah and could see why Phyllis and just about everybody else thought she was great. But I went on to explain I'd been a friend of the family for years, and when a member asked for a favor it wasn't easy to just say no.

"And look at it this way. If I don't take the job, somebody else will be called in and they'll be happy to take money for telling Marcia what she wants to hear. Maybe I can't convince her she's wrong, but I'd have a better chance than any stranger."

She thought that over silently for a few seconds and said okay, ask.

"Did P.J. come to your clinic about an impotency problem?"

"No."

"Would you know if he did?"

"Of course. This is a small office. Two doctors, four nurses, a receptionist and a part-time technician. Nobody comes in I don't see or at least know about."

"Whose idea was it for Sorah to visit Matt's cabin?"

"Mine. It was a natural. She likes swimming and water skiing and parties, and that's what Matt's place is all about. Jerry and I visit him often. I told Matt about her, he said he'd bring her, and he did."

I thanked her and said goodbye.

Matt and I discussed the dialogue, and it seemed apparent he was bothered by it. When probed, he finished his beer, went for another, brought two, handed me one and slouched in an easy chair.

"The truth," he said, "is that Sorah told me herself that she asked for the invitation. She'd heard about P.J. when there was a profile in the *Tribune* a while after Ma died, knew he was my father and that Jerry and Phyl now and then came to my place weekends. Obviously Phyl thinks you might make something of that, so she lied a little. What do you make of it?"

I said I'd think about it.

Chapter 4

Sandra came to the front door, blinked her big brown eyes while staring through the screen and asked if Matt would take her water skiing.

"How come I'm always the one?" he asked.

"Well, you're never busy and besides, you do it so good."

"No, I don't; I do it well. What's in it for me?"

She gave that a moment's thought and said he could watch.

"That's worth something," he granted, "but somebody's got to keep a lookout so we don't run over anybody."

Sandra glanced my way and smiled hopefully. "He can come along and do that."

Matt finally agreed on the condition that she quit without a squawk when he thought she'd had enough. She hopped up and down, making her double braids fly, told him he was so neat and raced for home. We followed at a more sober pace and I asked Matt when Sorah'd told him about her interest in his father.

"The second time she came out with Jerry and Phyl. We'd had a great day—taught her water skiing and after a late dinner we went for a walk along the shore under a full moon and I kissed her. She didn't resist, but the response was more polite than passionate. Hell, it wasn't even affectionate. And then she told me she was ashamed of herself for taking advantage of me. I asked what that meant and she laid it out. Nothing coy, believe me. I hate to tell you how pissed I got. Spouted all the obvious garbage—he was too old—why'd she want to take over nursemaiding a man who'd be in his dotage within a few years? All gracious as hell coming from a loyal son. I did manage to keep from accusing her of being after his money."

"Did you warn her that he was impotent?"

He looked at me, guessed where I'd heard that, and nodded sadly. "Wouldn't you?"

"I suppose so."

"Yeah, well, she said that made no difference. At the time I guessed that was part of the attraction; she was an orphan, probably been sexually abused as a kid. That's the usual theory these days, practically a cliché now, isn't it?"

"You really went for her, didn't you?"

He laughed a little too easily and said it was more a matter of deflated ego than heartbreak. Then we arrived at Luke's dock where Sandra waited, sitting on the far edge with her legs dangling over the water and her skis in place.

A few minutes later Matt eased Luke's red runabout with its thirty-horse Mercury around to the dock end, and handed the tow rope bar to Sandra. She clutched it, wriggled her tight little bottom to the dock edge, and Matt slowly moved us out. When the tow rope cleared the water, she yelled, "Hit it!" The motor roared, we leapt forward, and Sandra jerked the tow handle against her chest and was up and off.

Almost at once she cut to her right, leaning hard and throwing a wake higher than her small head. When she was far to our side, she abruptly cut back and began crisscrossing over our wake.

"How long's she been skiing?" I yelled at Matt.

"Since May of last year," he yelled back, grinning. "We'll swing around and she'll drop one of the skis."

With one ski she was even more impressive.

"She's so light we can get away with almost anything," Matt yelled at me. "If I tried her stuff that far to the sides this boat'd flip. Actually did once. Nearly ruined the motor."

Much later Matt made a long, sweeping turn back toward the dock and chopped the air with his right hand. Sandra threw up the tow handle, cut toward shore and gracefully sank into water up to her neck about three yards from the beach.

I coiled the tow rope as Matt edged us toward the dock.

"She's something, huh?" said Matt. "Worth watching. A complete natural."

"How was Sorah?" I asked.

"Not bad. And crazy eager. Stood around and got sunburned waiting for extra turns the first day she tried it."

"Nervy as Sandra?"

"Nobody but Luke is. But Sorah took a couple really good spills trying cuts she couldn't handle yet, and came back. She's a lot tougher than she looks."

Handy was up, dressed and eating an apple when we returned to the cabin. Ann Rose stood before a mirror on the northeast wall, stroking her thick dark hair. She concentrated on it, as though the brushing were a black magic ritual.

When Handy introduced her to Matt, she leaned forward to sight him in the mirror and smiled politely. When he introduced me, her hand stopped, she lowered the brush and turned around.

"Well, Kyle Champion, in the flesh. What a pleasant surprise."

"I didn't get your last name," I said.

"King. I remember you on TV. My favorite anchorman."

36

I thanked her and said actually my role was straight man for the brunette.

She laughed, turned back to the mirror and gave her hair a couple finishing licks with the brush. She was willowy in light gray slacks and a pale pink silk blouse. Her skin was pale and flawless except for a brown mole on her left temple. Her slender nose emphasized a wide, full-lipped mouth. The chin was a fraction too small, and she pushed it forward to compensate.

Matt asked if she were hungry and she said famished.

"What I want," she said, "is a big fat T-bone steak. I don't care if I never see another bit of fruit."

"I'll take you into Brainerd," said Handy.

"No need," said Matt. "I've got to pick up groceries anyway, and I'd like steak too. If they don't have T-bones will a sirloin do?"

"Dreamy," she said.

"Only if I buy," said Handy. "Ann Rose and I'll run over to Erickson's."

"Not me, Dearie. I want to clean up and change clothes."

"I'll wait."

"No, I don't want anybody stewing around expecting me to rush. You can handle it fine alone."

He stalled, watching her mournfully until she went into the bedroom and drew the curtain. After a moment he went to the door and said he wanted to talk with her.

"I'm changing clothes."

"Well, hold on a minute—"

"Do me a favor, Honey, get my bag from the car, okay?"

"I want to come in."

"I'm not decent. Be a dear and get the goddamned bag, will you?"

"Uh, yeah, sure."

He turned, red-faced, and signaled Matt to join him as he walked out through the kitchen. I was beginning to feel like a visible eavesdropper and wandered out the front door and down toward the lake. A few minutes later I heard Handy's car start and leave. Matt came down and joined me.

"Poor Handy," he said, "he's convinced Ann Rose has the hots for you."

"Tell him I'm already spoken for."

"I don't think he'd be impressed. He's a very insecure guy for all the muscle and grace."

We heard the front door slam and both looked up to see Ann Rose approaching in a powder blue robe and clogs. Her hair was rolled in a bun on her neck.

"Are there lots of people around the lake?" she asked as she came near.

"Not a lot, why?"

"I want to go in the water, but I don't have a suit with me. Would you guys mind going up in the cabin and not peeking?"

"We'll go up to the cabin," Matt assured her.

"Great."

We went. Inside he promptly produced a pair of military field glasses and went to the front window. Somehow I wasn't surprised, and I strongly suspected what he did was exactly what Ann Rose had figured on.

"This is the first time," said Matt, "that I've ever been sorry I never cleared out the trees between here and the beach."

We stood before the couch by the windows and saw Ann Rose step slowly into the water beside the dock. She was still wearing the robe which extended just below her knees, and pulled it up as she waded slowly into the water. When it reached her thighs she paused, studied the distant shore line, glanced left and right, slipped off the robe, dropped it on the deck and dove smoothly into the water.

"Swims beautifully for a girl raised in Iowa," observed Matt. "Good form. Nearly flawless. Wonder where she learned?"

"Maybe her parents threw her in the river when she was still a pup."

He chuckled and adjusted the focus.

Ann Rose reached the point across the small bay, turned around and sat in the water where it was deep enough to reach her shoulders.

"I'm afraid," said Matt, "that she's not a genuine exhibitionist."

Suddenly she started, glanced over her shoulder and abruptly launched herself forward. Her strokes were swift and rough with no posing. In a very few moments she was back to the dock where she snatched her robe, wrapped it around her and came trotting up to the cabin.

"There was a man in the woods," she said, breathing heavily, "looked like a tramp. What's a tramp doing here at the lake?"

Chapter 5

A little after five Matt made scotch and sodas for himself and Ann Rose, and a gin and tonic for me. Less than half way through her drink, Ann Rose was making fun of her panic over the tramp sighting.

"Actually," she admitted, "I took off so fast I never got a really clear view. He was probably as startled as I was and ran when I took my dive."

She'd put on blue tights, black pumps and a pale pink sweatshirt with a logo I couldn't catch but was certain didn't come from Penney's. Her legs looked as expensive as the sweatshirt.

When Handy arrived with the steaks, fresh fruit, yogurt and wheat bread, Matt went out to the kitchen and they started working on dinner.

I told Matt I thought I'd take a walk, and Ann Rose said that was a dandy idea, she'd come along. Matt caught my eye and suggested I wait, the steaks wouldn't take long, and we'd be eating in a few minutes. I sat down. Ann Rose turned sulky for a few seconds, suddenly got a sly look and started questioning me about my TV work and personalities I'd known. Before she got around to grilling me about my current activities, Matt broke in and asked her to set the table. She gave him a knowing look and did the job with more grace than I'd have expected.

All through the salad course she focused on me until I told her I'd appreciate it deeply if she'd knock off the interview. I was beginning to feel foolish trying to answer like a star when the TV schtick had just been a short, stupid side-track in my life.

She told me I was too modest. When she had started it all I'd thought she was really interested, but as the questions went on and I observed Handy's reactions, it became obvious she was simply torturing him. She overdid the vamping bit to the point where I felt she was not only punishing Handy because he bored her, but was needling me because I'd been famous in a less than honorable way. Until that meal I thought I'd never met a pretty woman I didn't like.

Ann Rose gave me a new perspective.

When the steak hit her plate her conversation lapsed. She ate with a fine, animal appetite.

Handy's refusal of wine distracted her briefly. She paused in her feeding frenzy to ask if his mother had told him one sip would give him delirium tremens or a ruined liver. He made no defense or explanation. I began to like him.

Eventually Matt took over the dialogue, which at least raised its level from his viewpoint.

After dinner three of us drank cointreau. I noticed that while Ann Rose had emptied her wine glass often and took two drinks before the meal, she seemed unaffected and enjoyed the liquor with relish.

It was about nine o'clock and light lingered on the lake when Sorah came to our door wearing white slacks and a blue turtleneck sweater.

Matt was so startled to see her, she apologized, saying she had to come because he didn't have a telephone, and she was inviting everyone to join at her house for poker.

Within half an hour we were seated around P.J.'s big

poker table, playing draw with four Kruegers, Handy, Ann Rose and me.

All of my family consider me impaired when it comes to poker. Something in my head rejects remembrance of cards held or seen, and while I can usually detect a bluff by average players, I never had a prayer with either my family or the Kruegers. They could all remember every card seen in a deal, and in an incredible percentage of the time, guessed the contents of opponents' hands by the set of a mouth, an intake of breath or a seemingly innocent comment. This I knew of Matt and Luke particularly. I wasn't so sure about Marcia, who hadn't often played with us, and of course Sorah was an unknown factor.

In the next two hours I learned Sorah was either a magician or luckier than hell, because she won not only consistently but flamboyantly. Marcia dropped out before me. Handy did relatively well, more often than not in hands where Sorah folded early. Ann Rose was about broke when I withdrew.

I made drinks for the players, talked briefly with Marcia and stepped outside. It was another moonless night and I could see northern lights flickering almost directly overhead, not the shifting, curling curtains I remembered in younger days, but more vaporous. Frogs were in full chorus around the lake.

After a few moments I walked in back of the cabin and started up the road that climbed a slope leading to the county road a ways north. I had gone half a dozen yards when I heard footsteps behind me and turned.

It was Ann Rose.

"I like an adventurous man," she said. "Where are we going?"

"Exploring. Thought I'd see if I could find the farm of a

madman who used to live what we used to call yonder."

She moved to my side and looked up at me quizzically. Her face had a lovely glow in the pale starlight. I wondered if I'd had too much to drink, because suddenly she seemed irresistible.

"Starlight becomes you, Mr. Champion," she said, as if guessing my inclinations.

"I hope," I said, "that you're not planning to get me knocked silly by your oversized boyfriend."

"Don't be afraid. Handy wouldn't dream of punching out a guy smaller than he is. You know he played professional football and quit because he didn't like hurting people?"

"No. I think you're bulshing me."

"Does that mean bullshitting? Come on, Kyle, don't give me baby talk. Anyway, I'm not kidding about Handy. There's nothing there for you to worry about."

I started walking and she kept up with me.

"Actually, Handy's a problem for me," she said. "My God, look at his body. Have you ever seen so much man? And he's not really a Neanderthal. I mean, he went to college and actually passed courses in stuff besides Phys-Ed. He likes history and he's read Hemingway and Jack London. He can't hack the heavyweights, let alone any current hotshots."

We were over the small hill and out of the woods surrounding the lake. Now crickets were louder than the frogs behind us, and the landscape seemed lighter under the enormous star-filled sky. Here the northern lights flickered more visibly. Ann Rose glanced up at it all and evidently felt it was intrusive.

"I hope," she said, "that you're not going to point out constellations."

"Couldn't if I wanted to."

"Do you really know where you're going right now?"

"Probably not. You don't have to come along, you know."

"I'd be afraid to go back alone now. Might get lost."

I turned west when we hit the road, and she stayed close as we hiked along the shallow ditch on the left side until we came to a shattered gate on the right. I paused, then drifted across the graveled road and on to the ruts leading north. A low shack came in sight and then a smaller one beyond it. We passed the concrete remnants of a barn that had gone down long before, and I began seeing litter several yards away from the shack.

Ann Rose gripped my arm.

"What is this? What're you looking for?"

"It's the farm a guy named Thorvald owned back when I came up here every summer. He was a bachelor who built the cabin you see over there and all the furniture in it. A genuine recluse."

"You think he was the one who was out on the point when I swam over there?"

"It can't be, if Matt's got the story right. Says he was killed in a bus accident some time ago."

"Then why are we here?"

"I'm here because your tramp reminded me of him, made me want to see the place."

"Okay, we've seen it. Let's go back."

"A little closer first."

"Oh hell," she responded, and started walking boldly toward the shack. I went with her and in a moment could see the machine shed and the overturned outhouse beyond.

We stopped in the cabin's front yard and stared at the sagging door, the broken windows and the littered yard.

The vandalization had been thorough and vicious. I saw a book at my feet and picked it up, but couldn't make out the title in the dim light. It appeared to be a text.

"You going inside?" she asked.

"No." The idea was too depressing.

She hugged my arm.

"It makes me melancholy," she whispered. "I want to cry. Please kiss me."

I looked into the glowing face held up vulnerably toward mine. A suspicion that she was deliberately manipulating me was strong, but when I put my fingertips on her cheek I felt a tear. Suddenly her hand was on the back of my head, she rose on tiptoe and kissed me firmly on the mouth. For a moment we held it, then she went on her heels, turned her head and clung to me a second before we broke and turned to head back.

I heard her gasp and my heart constricted painfully as we looked up and saw the man standing by the fallen gate. He leaned against the support post with one elbow resting on its top. His right arm dangled at his side.

"What'll we do?" whispered Ann Rose.

I gripped her hand while searching the ground for a weapon without lowering my head. There was nothing. I took a deep breath.

"We'll walk slowly past him and say good evening. If he comes toward us, move off. If I say run, go like hell and scream—okay?"

She nodded.

We walked toward the gate. A broad-brimmed hat obscured the face, but I could make out a scraggly beard and dark clothing. He was motionless.

We were within six feet of him when I said, "Good evening . . ."

45

He made no reply.

I walked on, holding Ann Rose's elbow firmly, keeping her on the side away from the man. I wanted to say "lovely night," or something equally innocent, but my throat was thick and I thought my voice might crack if I spoke again. We passed the gate walking at a steady pace while the sentinel turned, almost imperceptibly, watching our progress. I thought I saw the glitter of eyes under the hat brim, and then looked down at the dangling right arm and what hung from the hand. I tightened my grip on Ann Rose so hard she winced and reached up with her left hand to grasp my fingers.

We reached the road, crossed it listening to the sharp crunch of our footsteps and anticipating others in pursuit. There were none, but we increased our pace and at the edge of the wood began to run. I had a moment of panic when I thought I'd missed the rut road to Luke's, but soon realized we were okay and slowed a little. There was no sound from behind.

The moment we were in sight of the cabin, Ann Rose took off at a dead run and I followed her inside where she was already pouring out her fear on the people still seated around the poker table.

Handy was silent but his expression let me know he was sore that I'd endangered his love, and I couldn't help sympathizing with his anger. He walked her back to Matt's place ahead of us.

"It can't be Thorvald," said Matt. "I wonder if he had any relatives?"

"I don't think it was a ghost," I said.

He grinned. "Why not?"

"I saw what he was holding in his right hand, which he kept at his side almost out of sight. You ever hear of a ghost carrying a hatchet?"

46

Chapter 6

I woke about four, unhaunted by Thorvald's ghost but restless with concerns about Matt. Instead of showing sorrow or guilt about his lost father, he seemed angry. I knew when his former wife betrayed him he'd been morose and depressed, but he'd never shown obsessive jealousy or hatred. Maybe competing with his own father did it, but it still seemed out of character for him to nurse a grudge after the old man's sudden death.

I rolled out of the bunk, slipped into my moccasins and decided against using the indoor toilet. The walls were too thin and the flushing, I was sure, would raise the dead on such a quiet morning.

Outside the bedroom I stood a moment, listening to the hum of the refrigerator in the kitchen. There wasn't another sound in the cabin. On first retiring I'd listened to see if Ann Rose would take her giant lover to bed for safety's sake, but I'd heard him murmuring and then the bunk in his room next to mine groaned under his weight.

Apparently she had not been frightened enough to let him sleep with her. It was a bit disillusioning to me that he hadn't slept across her door. Perhaps there were limits to his chivalric impulses.

As I stepped into the parking area it occurred to me that venturing out where a madman with a hatchet might be loitering wasn't exactly a brilliant move, but too much drink and too little sleep combined to make me irrational. I figured if he showed I'd drown him.

The silence as I approached the old, rarely used outhouse, was almost palpable, and I longed for the sound of a loon or the cricket's chorus, but they had better sense than to be active at that hour.

The toilet smelled no sweeter than in the days when it was used regularly and I didn't linger. Feeling relieved but disarmed, I moved quickly back to the cabin as what I assumed was a truck drove along the county road behind me. It slowed and turned in to one of the lots east of P.J.'s white house.

I remembered that Peg, P.J.'s only daughter, and her husband Burt Beattie were supposed to show Friday night and wondered if it could be them. Back in bed my mind began imagining the late arrivals discovering the man with the hatchet at work on their cabin, or worse, waiting in ambush in the bedroom.

At five I dressed, went into the cold predawn light and walked briskly along the narrow path parallel with the lake until I'd passed the great white house, then the green log cabin and came to Burt's brown place at the eastern extreme of the Krueger holdings. A gray Winnebago, almost as big as a greyhound bus stood in the yard, and I saw light in the cabin's kitchen window. When I moved close, Peg's face appeared in it. She did a double-take and broke into a wide smile.

When we met at the back door she hugged me and said we'd have to whisper a while, Burt was still asleep in the bedroom and the kids were conked out in the Winnebago.

"We had a ghastly night," she told me. "Burt had a board meeting before we could take off, there was a big hassle and it didn't break up until after eleven. Then twelve miles this side of St. Cloud we had a flat tire. Can you imagine what that's like with our monster? One of the lugnuts was absolutely frozen and he couldn't get it loose.

So he called the triple A and couldn't get anyone forever and, oh Lord, it went on. How are you? Married or anything . . . ?"

"Sort of anything," I said, and told her about Megan and our French barge trip. She wanted details and absorbed them hungrily while we drank coffee at the kitchen table. Finally I moved the conversation to her family.

"Oh God," she sighed, "isn't it awful about Dad? And can you imagine him marrying practically a child bride? Have you met her?"

I nodded.

"Well then, you can see his side of it. I mean, she's beautiful, charming, smart . . . But his dying like that! No one can believe it really happened. Instead of just being broken up, we're all like stunned."

"Matt seems sore."

"Is that what you see? I suppose maybe you're right. He had a case on Sorah himself, you know. I'm afraid she rather raised hell with all of us when you come right down to it."

"Matt says P.J. embarrassed Burt."

"I hardly think that covers it. The greatest blow was when P.J. decided to leave everything to Sorah. He told the three of us the night when she had her miscarriage—didn't you know about that?"

"Hell no."

"It was early, nothing really traumatic but still upsetting because P.J. was terribly excited, and of course Sorah was too. She went into a sort of blue funk for a couple days. Anyway, we were at the house and P.J. told us about it and then said he planned to leave his estate to her intact. He said none of us needed any help, and he didn't want Sorah to feel she had to marry again. If she ever did have a child it should be well cared for, and he knew he wouldn't be around long enough to guarantee that."

"From all I've heard, I should think there'd have been plenty to go all around the clan."

"Of course. The truth is, he felt we all resented Sorah, and I hate to say it, but in a way, he held it against us that we all loved Mom more than him. And he felt guilty about being so happy with his new wife who never made fun of him and acted as if he were all that counted."

"You know what Marcia thinks?" I asked.

"Oh yes. That's why you're here, isn't it? To see if he died naturally. Burt says that's a joke. He says it's perfectly natural that a sixty-four-year-old man would die in bed with a twenty-four-year-old girl. As a matter of fact, he predicted it when they were married a year and a half ago. He said P.J.'d never make it back from England. He was awful."

"How's he now?"

"He's okay. Let's not talk about Burt."

She stared out the window at the pines beyond and sighed.

"P.J.'s insistence on no funeral or memorial service makes things worse. There's no ritualistic ending to tidy things up. Maybe that sounds stupid, but I can't help it; however ghastly funerals may be, they're needed. Without that ritual, death seems unreal and you can't adjust . . ."

"You seem to be weathering it quite well."

"Don't let me fool you. Right now I'm giddy with loss of sleep. I came all apart when I first heard he was gone. Just couldn't believe it. Later I kept telling myself he had a good life, did all the things he wanted to and ended up with a worshipful young wife he enjoyed his last eighteen months. For him it was the way to go. Can you imagine him enduring senility, dependence, all the humiliations decrepitude can bring? I watched Burt's father go through the nursing home thing and believe me, I sure wouldn't want to have seen any part of that for Dad."

"It sounds like you think he had a classy suicide."

"Well, why not? As far as I'm concerned, Sorah was good for him and I don't begrudge her a thing."

"Even if she got it all by calculation?"

"Oh pooh—I don't believe that a minute. Would you like an omelet or some scrambled eggs?"

I chose the omelet and got a dandy with melted cheese, chopped chives and a touch of thyme. Before we finished, seven-year-old Ted shuffled in and settled for an orange and cereal. Jimmy, who was five, came in while Ted was still sopping up sugared milk and wanted an omelet like mine. I had a moment of undivided attention when Peg told them I had been a regular on TV, but that evaporated when they learned it had been on a news show. I could only be grateful they weren't older. Teenagers would probably have sneered openly.

After they'd gone to the beach, I told Peg about the mysterious stranger who'd been hanging around, and suggested she warn the boys to avoid explorations into the surrounding woods during the day and any prowling at all during dark.

She wasn't unduly worried, and I left her stacking breakfast things in the dishwasher.

Strolling along the beach I sighted a young woman stroking a white rowboat toward the white house dock. Suddenly I recognized Sorah and walked to meet her. She smiled brilliantly, and a moment later nudged the prow close enough for me to reach down and pull the boat alongside.

"Get in," she said. "I'll show you the Sorah tour."

I did, shoved us clear and took the aft seat facing her as

she swung us about briskly and began stroking toward the point.

"I see you've already been visiting with Peg," she said. "When did they get in?"

I told her it was about four.

"My, you don't waste any time, do you?" She was still smiling.

"I don't sleep well," I said. "Woke early and when I heard them arrive imagined them finding their cabin vandalized, or worse, occupied by the guy Ann Rose and I saw last night. Couldn't get to sleep so I went over to check them out."

She stroked steadily but not with the sort of energy that would develop unsightly muscles. Her blue jeans were tight and handsome on her slender legs. Her feet were bare, and the nails were natural color but had a shine as if polished. A stylishly oversized white sweatshirt covered and concealed her torso. I could see the flash of her substantial engagement ring. The wedding band was wide and plain. She wore no other jewelry, not even a watch.

I asked what sort of nursing she'd done before her marriage, and she said she was an RN in a urology clinic.

"Is that where you met P.J.?"

"No, we met here at the lake. Matt introduced us; didn't he tell you?"

I admitted he had.

She lifted her chin slightly. "I suppose Marcia told you he had an impotency problem?"

I admitted that too.

"So what's your theory on why I married him?"

"I don't have any."

"Come on, you must've been working hard at trying to pick one. What's your first bet?"

"I'd guess you were looking for a father."

"Because I called him Daddy? That was a joke. When we were first seeing each other he was bossy, and I started say, 'Yes, Daddy' and even 'No, Daddy,' and it became a habit. He didn't encourage it at first, but when he found it irritated his sons, he became overfond of it and I quit. It never pleased me to offend the family."

"Did Matt and P.J. quarrel over you?"

"It never came out in the open. At least not in my hearing, and neither one of them ever mentioned a quarrel. I sometimes think it'd have been better if they'd had it out. Matt was very hurt when I first told him I was seriously interested in his father."

"How'd you enjoy your trip to England?"

"Adored it. You've no idea what a joy it can be for a woman who's been a nurse to find herself being treated like royalty, living in luxurious hotels, eating dreamy meals and enjoying wonderful wines and all that."

"How'd people who knew his first wife react to you?"

She laughed and rested the oars.

"I think you could say, with studied politeness. Occasional rather subtle condescension. Most of the people I met were quite intelligent, and P.J. made it clear from the start, wherever we were, that he wouldn't tolerate snobbery toward me. He was prickly protective. I guess you know how formidable he could be. Much of the time I was treated like a charming pet. I don't believe we ever met a man who wasn't entranced by the spring/winter romance. Occasionally, women couldn't quite conceal their disapproval. I never saw those types more than once. P.J. claimed they were all wives of men dying with envy of him."

She resumed rowing and took us around to the bay where I'd fished with Matt the day before. He was there now with Handy. Both were casting along the edge of the lily pond. Matt saw us first and his eyebrows lifted before he managed to grin.

Sorah twisted around and asked if they were having any luck. Handy reached back for the stringer, lifted it high and showed us three lovely bass.

"It's two to one, in his favor," said Handy.

"Where's Ann Rose?" asked Sorah.

"Still in the bunk, the last I know."

"Did she sleep badly after the scare?"

"I didn't hear her moving around. She usually sleeps heavy."

"We'll go check on her," said Sorah, and began swinging us around. Matt, who'd wound in his line during the exchange, sat holding the rod lightly and watching Sorah. She nodded her head at him and pulled stoutly on the oars. I looked back as Handy made a long cast that landed between two lily pads. Matt kept watching us soberly.

"Really," said Sorah when we were out of hearing, "can you imagine those two louts going off and leaving that girl alone in the cabin after last night's scare? If she gets up and finds herself alone, she'll be mad and I wouldn't blame her."

I just hoped she was alone.

Chapter 7

The cabin looked serene as we approached after tying up the rowboat at the dock, but I'd caught Sorah's apprehension, and we raced up the path to the front door. I reached it first and charged through to the addition. Nothing looked out of order, so I stopped at the curtain across Ann Rose's door and turned to Sorah. She slipped past me and peered inside.

"Ann Rose?" she said.

There was no response. Sorah pushed the curtain aside and stepped through. I heard a grunt, then an angry, "Leave me alone!"

Sorah came out grinning.

"She's alive but not awfully happy about it. Handy's right, she's a heavy sleeper. I think she dies a little."

She led me back to the kitchen, found coffee still hot on the warming burner, poured for both of us, and we sat beside the fireplace. She lifted her cup to me.

"Cheers."

After a sip she cradled the cup in her lap and tilted her head against the high back.

"What made you wander up to Thorvald's farm last night with her?"

"Going with her wasn't my idea. She just horned in. I went because I felt sorry for the guy and wanted a look at his place."

"Did you kiss her before you saw the ghost?"

I felt the warmth of flushed cheeks and decided there was no point in lying.

"Was it obvious to everyone?"

"It was to me. The smudge was faint, but unmistakable. She doesn't seem your type, somehow."

I tasted the coffee, which had been on the heat too long, and crossed my legs.

"What do you figure is my type?"

She laughed easily. "I've no idea, really. Would you like me to leave you on guard here?"

"I'd appreciate the hell out of it if you'd stay right here."

"All right," she said, getting up, "in that case I'll make fresh coffee. This stuff is awful."

Ann Rose appeared about half an hour later, tousle-headed and wearing her powder-blue robe and clogs. Her eyes widened at the sight of Sorah and me in the kitchen, and looked around as if she thought she'd awakened in the wrong cabin.

Sorah offered her orange juice. She accepted it without thanks and carried her glass off to the bathroom.

"Not at her best when first up," said Sorah, "but then, who is?"

I thought I might be but didn't mention it, knowing it wouldn't win any points, and told her the coffee was a great improvement over Matt's.

Ann Rose returned eventually, wearing white shorts and a black tank top which fit like a condom. Her breasts looked neat and I guessed would be pointy when free of the binding. She had brushed her lush hair, put on lipstick and touched up her eyes with a hint of liner.

"Well," she said, "how nice of you to come, as the hero told the tart; now if I can have some coffee I'll manage to be human."

She wanted no breakfast and asked if either of us had a cigarette. We didn't, and she made a face suggesting that was about what one might expect in this company.

"I didn't notice you smoking last night," said Sorah.

"I quit on the trip with the muscle. He's allergic, can you imagine? A monster like that and a little smoke reduces him to sneezes, wheezing and tears. God. Listen, I want to get something straight. Did you really marry the old man—P.J. was it?"

"Yes," said Sorah. "I really did."

"Wow, what are you—about twenty?"

"Twenty-three. I'll be twenty-four in August."

"Fandamntastic! And he was what? Seventy-five?"

"Merely sixty-four. We were only forty years apart."

"Oh well, that's hardly worth mentioning." Ann Rose drank, watching Sorah over the cup rim. She grinned when she lowered it.

"And eighteen months after the wedding he died and you're an heiress. Wonderful. What's next, Donald Trump?"

"I haven't thought about it yet." Sorah smiled at Ann Rose, and I felt they were playing a game I couldn't follow.

"Why'd you kiss Kyle last night?" Sorah asked.

Ann Rose looked at me. They both did.

"I'm not really sure. It just seemed like a good idea at the time."

"You really don't know why?"

"Well, the place was really depressing. I mean, you could see it'd been somebody's home. Guys had torn it all up, and it was nothing to begin with. All of a sudden I felt sad as hell, and he seemed sad too, so I felt maybe a kiss'd make us think of something else."

"Did it?"

"Who knows? We spotted the spook immediately after, and that sort of loused up my analyzing the situation."

"Why'd you kiss back?" Sorah asked me.

I shrugged and Ann Rose laughed. "He's one of those compulsively polite types. What else could he do?"

Suddenly they both lost interest in me and stared at each other.

"Are you staying for the memorial party on Monday?" asked Sorah.

Ann Rose lowered her coffee cup to the table and suddenly looked depressed.

"I don't know. I just don't know what the hell I want to do right now. Isn't it a family thing?"

"You'd be welcome."

"I know old Handy's practically family to Matt, but I'm not. I wouldn't fit in. The awful truth is, sweet guys aren't my bag and Handy's so sweet he makes me sick, and that turns me bitchy, and that turns everybody off me. Sometimes I think I ought to just stick my head in a plastic bag."

"What made you think you wanted to marry Handy?"

"It would have zonked out my old man. But the trouble is, marrying Handy wouldn't be worth it."

She discovered me again.

"Hey, Kyle, baby, you've got a car. How about getting me some cigarettes?"

"I'm afraid you'd think I was trying to be sweet."

"No I won't. I'll think you're a prick because you'd do a thing that'd get poor old Handy sneezing his ass off. Do it. I'll pay you back and cover a six-pack of beer as a bribe."

"Sorry. You'd talk about me while I was gone."

"Not to worry. We'll forget you exist until you get back."

I went and got her a package of Benson and Hedges. When I returned they were still sitting with coffee. Rose told me she owed me, but didn't pay.

"Hey," she said, "how'd you know my brand?"

"I didn't figure you for a Marlboro man."

"I could go for this guy," Ann Rose told Sorah. "You ought to consider him yourself. The right kind of woman might shove him back into the big time. But I'm forgetting, you're a girl who picks 'em ready made, right?"

"I'm a girl who has to do some arranging for a party this Monday," said Sorah getting up. "Come back to my place with me and Estelle will make you some breakfast—I'll bet you're ready to eat now?"

"My God," Ann Rose told me, "this woman's a fairy godmother. I'm going to stick with her forever."

I watched them walking down the path to the dock and marveled at Sorah's tolerance and Ann Rose's gall. Ann Rose lacked Sorah's grace in entering the rowboat but managed to look prim as the widow manned the oars and started rowing them back home.

Try as I might, I couldn't figure those two women as just a couple of independent spirits who'd discovered each other, but had no idea what they might be up to.

Chapter 8

Handy interrupted my reading the *Second Rumpole Omnibus* when he entered the front door just before noon.

"Where's Ann Rose?" he asked gently.

"Up at Sorah's."

He nodded, walked into the other room and made a tour to be certain she had really left. After a few moments the toilet flushed; he came past me and entered the kitchen.

"How was the fishing?" I asked.

"Fine." He ran water in the sink a moment, filled a glass, drank and came back beside me.

"What I'd like," he said, "is for you to show me where you saw the man last night. You and Ann Rose."

"Why?"

"Want to see if he's hanging around there. I don't like him scaring people, and Matt says you saw he had a hatchet. Might be dangerous."

"Which is a good reason for not going around to bug him on his own ground."

"I won't bug him. Just want to look for myself. You scared?"

"You bet. But if you like, fine, let's go. What's Matt doing?"

"Cleaning fish."

"He know where we're going?"

"Uh-huh."

As we went through the porch, he picked up a sturdy cane leaning against the wall. I asked if he had a bad leg. He said no.

We walked along the rutted road with him in the left track and me in the right. Biting flies the Kruegers called delta-wings came to buzz around our heads. It always seemed to me that these pests were assigned by some hostile force to harass nature lovers, one per walker. If you managed to kill one, and that was possible if you didn't mind half beating your brains out trying to smack them when they landed, another was immediately assigned to take the dead one's place.

Handy ignored his fly. I guessed his thick hide was immune to insect bites.

We crossed the county road, walked through the ruined gate and approached the vandalized shack. It was a dispiriting sight in daylight. We could see litter: pots and pans, cans, torn up magazines, and vandalized books. I stooped to pick up a book and read the title: *Economic Principles*.

"No wonder he went nuts," I thought, and put the book back on the gravelly earth.

The ramshackle house had simulated brick siding and a tarpaper roof. The windows were blank and strips of siding had fallen or been torn off, revealing patches of tarpaper and raw wood. We moved closer and saw bits of furniture strewn around the lot among broken crockery and more paper. Handy pulled the sagging front door open enough to slip through sideways, while I stood outside, staring at the desolation.

"Nobody's been living in there," he said when he emerged.

"Is his homemade, galvanized sink still intact?" I asked.

He shot a quick glance my way that suggested surprise, but his face kept the blankness it always offered me.

"Yeah. You looked inside before?"

"Matt described it to me. He came around the year after

Thorvald was committed, before vandals got at it."

Handy nodded and stared toward the nearby machine shed.

"Guy must've put a lot of work on the place. Everything handmade. Crude, but solid. Hell of a thing to wreck it all like that. No excuse in the world."

"What'd you do if you caught vandals wrecking a place of yours?" I asked.

"Probably kill 'em," he said, without a hint of anger or malice. It was a simple statement of fact. He didn't even grip the cane he was carrying with any greater force that I could see.

"Where'd you meet Ann Rose?" I asked.

He started walking toward the machine shed and spoke without turning his head my way.

"I don't want to talk about Ann Rose with you. Okay?"

I said fine and followed him to the shed.

It had a dirt floor littered with remnants of hay, and a small platform overhead extended half the length of the structure. By rising on his toes, Handy could peer into it, but it took a couple steps up the built-in ladder for a better look and a moment later he stepped down.

"Must have been sleeping there. Got an old blanket on some hay. Kept him out of the rain."

"If it's really Thorvald's ghost, he wouldn't need a blanket."

"I don't believe in ghosts. Either he didn't die, or he had a relative or friend."

We went farther north, and he paused at the corner of a concrete slab near the edge of the open field west of the shack.

"There was a small barn here once," he said with a wave of his hand. He gazed at the drains that had run behind stalls where cows once stood chewing their cuds while being milked. Dry wind swept over the open field, ruffling his straw-colored hair as he took in the pine trees standing tall against the clear sky.

Finally he cut straight back toward the county road, avoiding the vandalized shack. We pushed through tall billowing grass and scrubby brush which bobbed in the wind. The sun felt warm and the air smelled of fresh earth and pines.

"You mind talking about why you quit pro football?" I asked.

He didn't answer until we came to a barbed-wire fence separating us from the road. There he moved halfway between two posts, put his big foot on the lower strand, gripped the middle one, pulled it up to and beyond the top strand and tilted his head at me. I ducked through, then held it for him.

"It was partly something a Minnesota politician named Gene McCarthy said some time ago and I read about later. He said being a politician was like being a football coach. You had to be smart enough to know how to play the game, and dumb enough to think it was important."

"That's damned good."

"It made me think. I learned that to be any good as a pro you had to think it was important enough to kill or die for. I know almost any of the All Stars demonstrate that they have to believe that. If they didn't, they couldn't compete with guys that go nuts every Sunday and most of the days of the week through entire football careers. I just decided that for me, it wasn't that important."

"So what are you going to do next?"

"I'm working on it."

Chapter 9

Matt began fixing lunch while I described our visit to Thorvald's shack, and Handy went up to the white house to see if Ann Rose would be eating with us. I ended my account with Handy's quote from Gene McCarthy. Matt grinned.

"So now you know he's not all muscle, huh?"

"If he's really got a mind, how come he takes so much guff from Ann Rose?"

"I've made a personal investigation of that subject and discovered, admittedly on the basis of limited resources, that men who won't take guff from women are usually morons or tyrants."

Handy interrupted our discussion with the news that Ann Rose wasn't joining us.

I was relieved and thought Matt felt the same way, but it surprised me when Handy's attitude suggested he was too.

We ate the bass they'd caught, and after some idle chatter Matt told Handy about Marcia's theory of P.J.'s death. He presented it as if he were seeking Handy's opinion. As far as I could tell, Handy's attention never wavered from his meal, but when he was through eating he settled back, drank the last of his milk and asked where P.J. had died.

"In his bed at the white house."

"Was Sorah with him?" I asked.

"No. She says she found him dead when she came out of the bathroom."

"What time?"

"About ten-thirty."

"Who else was in the house?" I asked.

"Luke, Marcia, Burt, Peg, me . . ."

"Was Jerry at your cabin that weekend?"

"Yeah."

"But he didn't come to the poker party?"

"He never went near the white house from the time he ran away at fourteen. If we went out on the lake, he didn't even look up toward it."

Matt said that with a pained expression, and abruptly rose to pour fresh coffee for us.

"What about Estelle?" asked Handy. "Was she still up when P.J. died?"

"No. She'd gone to bed well before."

"How come all the family was still around when P.J. and Sorah had gone to their room?" I asked.

"Oh, that wasn't unusual. We had a poker game going and P.J. told us to stay with it. He'd done that before since marrying Sorah."

He laughed shortly. "Marcia said once she thought he did it to make his sons envious."

I was sure it did.

We picked up our dishes, carried them to the kitchen and Matt washed while I dried. He banished Handy, saying he was too big for the space and the big man drifted outside.

"What was the atmosphere like just before P.J. died?" I asked. "Any tension, antagonism . . . ?"

"No. Everything was very normal. There wasn't a lot of kidding during the game when he played with us, not as far back as I can remember. The problem was way deep. He resented it that none of us picked him as a model. He wanted us to join the family business, expand his empire, establish a damned dynasty. It galled him we were interested in things that bored him. I read fiction and even studied philosophy, Luke's a classical music nut and an opera lover. Peg married a guy P.J. figured was nothing but a well-dressed beggar, and he never talked about Jerry. He was too far out for P.J. to even think about. The old man wanted us to be business majors, or at least lawyers or accountants, something useful in what he considered the real world. He took our career choices as a slap in the face, spit in the eye. He thought we felt superior, too good for him. We were unnatural children. He even resented our water skiing and playing badminton. It was only natural that when Sorah showed up and found him more interesting than me, he thought that proved something. She was the first person in his life he was sure appreciated him enough. I think he blamed Ma for the directions we took. She was supposed to be awed by his genius for moneymaking and impressing important people. She never bought any of that. And all of a sudden he had Sorah who gave him everything he ever wanted. She took him seriously. Ma never could, and he supposed we felt the same."

By this time I had hung up the towel and was just watching him. He put the frying pan on a shelf in a cabinet beside the sink and straightened up with a rueful smile.

"I don't know what offended him most, my becoming a professor, or Peg marrying a guy involved with charities. He didn't mind Luke's field so much, figured there was a potential for money there and maybe even power, but it smacked of ideas, writing, and what he called butt-kissing. That's what public relations people were to P.J. Professional butt kissers."

"Did Burt hit him up for contributions to the U.?"

"Only once. Burt started the approach with questions

about P.J.'s business, his techniques, priorities, marketing strategies. All stuff that sounded as it he were dying to learn the magic. And then he started working around to what interested P.J. outside of business, and he couldn't find anything, so he moved to how P.J. wanted to be remembered. In about three seconds flat the old man wised up to the fact he was going to be asked for big money in exchange for immortality through a foundation in his name doing good works through all time. P.J. told him to take a walk."

With the kitchen all in order he led me outside, where we found Handy on the dock. Matt suggested we go water skiing.

"We'll use Burt's boat," said Matt. "Luke's probably couldn't pull Handy off the dock."

Burt was up and wearing long, stylish trunks in a red flower pattern. He looked like swimming suit models drawn for the *Saturday Evening Post* back in the forties, except his head was covered with black curls, and he wasn't quite five-feet-eight inches tall. His voice was deep and rich, and he asked where I'd been in France, how the people treated me and probed for specific answers. I thought of him talking with P.J. and wondered if he thought, because I'd been on TV, I might have a lot of money. Then I felt chintzy about suspecting his motives. His sincerity seemed too real to be faked.

The skiing went well. Burt ran his boat sensibly, without excessive flourishes, and let each skier make the most of his talents. Handy was skillful but unexpectedly cautious, Matt was a smooth professional, and the best I could say for myself was that I took only one spill, got tired and had fun. After my run Burt told me my fall was the good kind—I'd tried a tricky cut and missed. Nothing to be ashamed of. Since I had no illusions about my skill, I hadn't been ashamed but felt his assurances were thoughtful.

Peg came down to the dock while Matt was towing Burt and watched the show with me. Handy was riding in the power boat beside Matt, serving as a lookout for other craft and stray swimmers.

"Burt's really good," I told Peg.

"Yes," she said, a little vacantly, "he has to be. Listen, I want you all to come here for dinner tonight. You could stand a change in menu and I'm making spaghetti. Tell Matt to bring a red wine, will you?"

I agreed, and when she still lingered, told her I'd been talking with Matt about her father and how things were after his second marriage.

"According to Matt, none of his offspring had anything in common with him. How come you all wound up with cabins along this lake? Why did P.J. want a place here?"

At first I thought she wasn't willing to discuss it, but after a moment's thought she answered.

"Well, he loved fishing. That was probably the start of it. Then he bought this stretch of beach back when he thought he could hold the family all together. I think he imagined something like an ongoing seminar, or more likely, an ongoing business conference with worshipful offspring listening to Daddy by the lake around a bonfire. That didn't happen."

She stared across the water beyond the boat and skier, took a deep breath and focused on me.

"So, what's with your love life?"

"It'd bore you."

"Come on, tell me."

"It went kaput. The dream blonde fell in love with a career."

"Poor Kyle. Up against an unbeatable rival."

She looked out at the lake again, and it occurred to me I'd never paid attention to her looks. She was the tomboy kid sister with a perky grin and flying pigtails when I first knew her. Now I saw her lovely profile with its stylishly pug nose, large eyes, high forehead and strong chin. She turned to smile at me warmly.

"Did you know I had a crush on you back when you came to the lake for the first time with Matt?"

I couldn't have been more startled if she'd kissed me. At the time she mentioned, she'd been about sixteen, and was already establishing a reputation as an athlete, competing in tennis, volleyball and swimming. From all I'd heard she'd been more likely to wrestle boys then neck with them, and I couldn't imagine her mooning over her older brother's friend.

Now she was a very feminine woman in faded blue jeans and a red halter top that modestly covered neat small breasts. Her bare shoulders and midriff were smooth and golden with tan.

I admitted my surprise.

"You were the only guy Matt ever brought around who really noticed me. All the two weeks you were here, I got breathless every time you glanced at me, and when you smiled, I thought I'd die. Am I embarrassing you?"

I laughed and admitted she was.

"Well," she said kindly, "don't worry. I got over it. But I'm glad you're here. It makes me think of some happy moments in a time when I thought I was mostly miserable. See you at dinner."

And she walked up to her cabin.

Chapter 10

Sorah and Ann Rose joined me on the dock while Burt was still skiing. Both wore bathing suits, so I assumed Sorah had loaned one of hers to the visitor. The amount of material involved wouldn't fill a matchbox and served more as decoration than cover. Sorah had the advantage; her skin glowed with a coppery tan covering every inch of her exposed body. Beside her, Ann Rose seemed pale, and her borrowed bikini revealed chalky areas bordering the bottom. Her buns, compared with Sorah's, looked boyish.

"Who's on the skis?" Ann Rose asked me.

"Burt," said Sorah. "You met him at the poker party."

"Oh sure. The gorgeous little man. He must ski a lot, huh?"

When Burt came in and joined us a few moments later, Ann Rose turned shy. I guessed she felt vulnerable in the bikini that showed her untanned hips.

Burt greeted the women warmly and offered to take either or both out for a ski run. Sorah deferred to Ann Rose, who shook her head almost desperately and said, "No, you go."

When Matt pulled the boat up beside us, Handy got out and told Ann Rose she'd have to be careful about getting burned.

"Don't sweat, Dearie," she said. "I'm all oiled and screened."

It came to me she wasn't suddenly shy; she'd decided to work at being charming because she wanted to stay.

"We've had a nice talk," Sorah told Handy, "and I've

asked Ann Rose to stay through the weekend and join in the memorial party on the Fourth—if that's all right with you."

Handy looked at Ann Rose whose face was glowing and said sure, if it wouldn't be any intrusion.

"Honey," said Ann Rose with thinly veiled asperity, "if she thought it was an intrusion she wouldn't have asked."

"Right," said Sorah. "You can both stay in my place; I've loads of room."

Matt, in response to Handy's apologetic glance, assured him it was the best plan. I didn't think it was for Handy, but had no chance to say so until after Sorah'd taken off on the skis with Burt driving the power boat and her two new visitors riding as passengers.

"He'll manage," said Matt when I'd had my say. "And maybe, living that close, he'll face the fact she's a little bitch and dump her. What I can't figure is why Sorah seems to find her so damned interesting."

"You think Sorah might like girls?"

"Not that way, no."

I asked if Sorah and P.J. had any differences he knew of, and he said not that anyone ever noticed. That was what galled Marcia most of all. She said the relationship had to be phony—no two people under any real circumstances could be so ungodly happy with each other. Especially when you considered the wild disparity in ages and background.

"And," continued Matt, "in Marcia's view, if the love was all that great, Sorah should've committed *suttee* when P.J. passed on."

"That'd be tough to do with his body turned over to the research department at the U. Which, incidentally, is pretty weird when you consider Burt trying to get money from the old man for the University Foundation, and all he'd give was his corpse. You think that was a deliberate slap?"

71

He gave me a wry look. "I thought only I had an imagination perverted enough to think of that. Far as I can tell, the notion hasn't occurred to Burt. He's not really long on imagination, and you've got to admit the idea's a stretcher. But it's exactly the sort of thing P.J.'d think of."

"Did you ever really like P.J.?"

He touched his goatee, then the mustache, and sighed.

"I admired him when I was a kid. I suppose it approached something like worship, in fact. He was the only God I ever believed in. But no, liking was never involved. My primary fear was of disapproval. He struck me once. I was thirteen. Luke and I'd been playing in the woods behind our house in Edina. He wouldn't quit horsing around when I was trying to build a lean-to. I told him to cut it out, he got snotty, and I whopped him one. Open handed. I think he was more startled than hurt. He ran to the house howling. P.J. asked him why, and he said I'd hit him. When I came back to the house P.J. met me at the door and said, 'Did you hit that kid?'

"I looked him in the eye and said yes. He slapped me. I saw it coming and stood up to it, and I kid you not, I saw stars. It was the greatest shock of my life. And he asked, 'How'd you like that?' I said I didn't like it at all. He asked what was I going to do about it. I said nothing and he asked why not, and I said because he was bigger than me. He said, 'You got the point. Don't ever forget it. And don't ever hit that kid again 'til he's as big as you.' "

We changed from swimming trunks to slacks, knit shirts and deck shoes before hiking back to Peg and Burt's place. The house smelled richly of Bolognese sauce, and Burt offered drinks at the small bar in the dining room. Peg told me Sorah had called to say she thought it'd be better if she took her guests into town since Handy wouldn't eat anything with red meat. Besides, the extra two would complicate seating arrangements in the dining room.

Peg said she knew Sorah well enough not to try and argue.

Matt opened the Chianti Classico he'd brought and poured for us often. We each had chunks of hot French bread, carrot sticks, radishes and sliced sun chokes dipped in buttermilk ranch dressing to go with piles of spaghetti and meat sauce.

The four kids ate in the kitchen, and Peg kept busy moving back and forth between the tables. We were almost through the meal before I realized the relationship between Peg and Burt was polite in a manner more natural between heads of state than a married couple. I remembered Burt believed in taking the host role seriously, as though by the numbers. This evening he was overdoing it, always offering to pass something, asking earnest questions, expressing his pleasure with the company and making complimentary comments on his wife's cooking and character.

Peg suggested that he relax a little.

Burt frowned at her and asked if she wanted some more spaghetti. She didn't look down at her half-filled plate as she smiled and shook her head, thanking him.

When there was a mild crash in the kitchen, Burt waved Peg back in her chair and charged out. We heard him chastising someone in a firm, low voice. Peg drank wine, set her glass down and smiled at me.

"Part of our problem," she said, "is that we don't really know what to expect Monday. Probably nothing awfully grand. But Sorah's making such a big deal of what she keeps calling a wake that we can't just relax and take whatever comes."

"What's insufferable," said Marcia, "is that she's running the whole business herself. It doesn't occur to her this family had an emotional investment all their lives in a man she knew less than two years. His natural children ought to have some say in how he's remembered, honored, or what-have-you."

"Yes," said Peg, "especially, 'what-have-you.' "

"Marcia," said Matt, "if she didn't give a damn about our feelings, she could've taken her inheritance, left the lake, Minnesota, and all of us, and gone to any paradise she wanted."

"Don't think she won't," said Marcia. "But first she'll rub our noses in the fact she was able to make him disinherit us for not fawning and welcoming her with open arms. She's never forgiven us for our disapproval, and I'd think you'd be the last to defend her the way she used you."

"Marcia," said Luke, "let's just knock it off, okay?"

"Yes," she said, reaching for the wine, "of course."

After dinner Burt served Kahlua topped with heavy cream in small, clear glasses with a teardrop base. When he left the table, Marcia took her two kids back to their cabin, Peg put the boys to bed, and Burt began cleaning up dishes after shooing us all out. Peg suggested we sit on the dock and watch stars. Their dock had a T-shaped ending and we sat in a row with Peg between Matt and me and Luke beside Matt. Pretty soon the brothers decided to take a boat ride, and I was alone with Peg.

"I guess," she said, "you're wondering why I arranged this meeting."

"Some."

She braced her hands on the dock edge and leaned forward, looking into the black water.

"I think Burt's fooling around."

It didn't seem she was expecting any comment and I made none.

"I'm not sure how long it's been going on, but it seems six months or so. That'd be about eight months after P.J. and Sorah came back from England."

"You think it's Sorah?"

"I'm not sure. Actually Burt had a little fling about two years ago. That petered out, if you'll pardon the expression. I don't think he went back to that one, but in his work he meets lots of high-powered, ambitious women, so there are plenty of chances. I just can't ignore the fact that Sorah knocked him out from the start, and then suddenly he was horribly indignant about her marrying Dad, and I got suspicious. He overdoes things when he's feeling defensive."

She was silent for a moment while we listened to bullfrogs and then a loon called. The lonely sound brought a pained expression that went as quickly as the call itself. She turned to me.

"I know it's not fair to throw this in your lap, but you've always been very special to me, and I know you're smart about people and I'm desperate."

"Did Matt suggest you talk with me?"

"No. I just told him I wanted to be alone with you, and he looked shocked, but shrugged and said okay. He probably thinks I intend to get even with Burt, but actually I'm just asking for help. From what you've seen so far, do you think it's Sorah?"

"No."

"Why?"

"She doesn't go for young men. She didn't go for Matt, why'd Burt appeal to her?"

"Well, Matt's probably the most interesting person in our family, but he's terribly detached, you know? I mean, he doesn't commit himself to one woman the way most of us want—or at least he hasn't been able to since his wife did him dirt. It doesn't make any difference who the woman is anyway. Although it'd be particularly ugly if it were Sorah. But I want to know what's going on and get enough evidence so when I cut the line I know what I'm doing. I can't go on with this crud—"

She started to cry and when I put my arm around her she took my hand and clutched it.

And then I felt a step on the dock and jerked away guiltily, turned and saw the night prowler crouching on the first section of the dock twenty feet away from us.

Chapter 11

Peg, who had turned with me, drew in a sharp breath, whispered, "Don't move," and scrambled to her feet.

"Thorvald?"

The man turned his head quickly to check the cabin, then moved in a crouch a few steps closer. I removed Peg's hand from my shoulder and stood.

"We heard you were dead," Peg told him.

"Who's he?" demanded the man, jerking his gaunt head at me. His voice almost creaked.

"Kyle Champion, an old friend of Matt's."

"He been snoopin' round. Tell 'im quit."

"All right. He doesn't want to bother you. We thought you were dead and he went up to look at your place. It upset him that somebody had wrecked it like that . . ."

He gestured impatiently and Peg shut up.

"Your pa dead?" he asked.

"Yes."

He nodded, turned and started off.

"Thorvald," Peg cried.

He reached the woods and disappeared.

"Damn," she muttered.

"How'd you know each other?" I asked.

"Oh," she said, waving her hand as she turned back to me, "it was nothing. I went to his place after P.J. put the police on him for killing Patsy. I've had enough woodchucks and raccoons in my garden to understand how upset a farmer gets over things that chew up what he's raised. I told him how I felt and gave him enough money for his fine.

P.J. knew I did it because I told him, thinking he might give the money back, but he didn't. He said I was a fool."

"You really talked with Thorvald?"

"Well, it was hardly a cozy chat. I told him why I was paying the fine. He grunted a few times and when I left walked to the gate with me. I offered my hand and he took it, and then he told me P.J. owed him for the chickens his dog had killed. You can imagine what a fool I felt after playing lady bountiful. I managed to keep from showing how mad I was that he'd try to get more from me but later I saw it differently.

"He wasn't greedy, he just figured fair was fair and he had it coming. The only trouble with that is, I'm not at all sure the dog killed any of his chickens. Maybe she upset them so they couldn't lay or something. Do you know if that happens? Anyway, Thorvald didn't forgive or forget, and I'm sure he's happy P.J.'s dead. He's obviously not right in the head, you know? It was only a week or so after that he shot at the hunters."

It seemed to me a mentally disturbed man could go over the edge if subjected to the treatment Thorvald had from the authorities and his neighbors, and I said nothing about the threat he still might be to her family other than to suggest again that the children be closely watched during their stay at the lake. And then I told her of seeing him holding a hatchet earlier.

That bothered her, but she said she couldn't believe he'd ever do anything to harm her, and I told her not to bet the kids' lives on it.

As we approached the cabin, she asked me not to tell Burt what happened. I agreed, said good night at her door and drifted up to the white house to see if Sorah and her guests were back.

They weren't. Estelle told me they planned to see a movie and she didn't expect them back before midnight.

I saw Matt through the window of Luke's place, joined them and reported on the latest Thorvald sighting. That started a lot of discussion, including the question of whether they were obligated to inform proper authorities that their ward wasn't dead, but alive and active. Luke was strongly for informing, Matt was opposed and Marcia wasn't much interested. What she wanted to know was how I happened to be alone with Peg on the dock.

She didn't pose the question that directly, but her curiosity and disapproval were evident, and I guessed she'd been aware of Peg's teenage crush. It didn't take long for me to decide I'd rather she knew the facts than suspect ill of Peg or me, and I said she wanted to ask me to check out something for her.

"What?" asked Marcia, with lofty eyebrows.

"Burt."

She stared at me with an expression somewhere between scorn and skepticism.

"You mean she thinks he's an imposter?"

"Hardly. She think he's been fooling around."

Marcia smiled with a sudden warmth and settled back on the couch. "Don't tell me; she suspects something between him and Sorah, right?"

"Why'd you think that?"

"Why not? Like all you men, he was obviously entranced the first time he saw the woman. He fumbled around calf-eyed until he discovered she was going to marry P.J., and then he was all outrage and indignation. While they were off to England, I thought he was planning to burn her as a witch when they returned. Instead, he became the loving brother-in-law. Did you notice his attitude toward me at dinner tonight when I became a touch catty about the dear?"

"I think that's nonsense," said Matt. "They've had absolutely no opportunity for hanky-panky."

"Maybe not here at the lake," admitted Marcia, "but can you account for either of them in Minneapolis?"

"She's been living here."

"Well yes, dear, I'm aware, but it's only a three-hour drive. And there's an old saying, 'Lust will find a way.' "

"I always thought that was love," said Luke.

"Don't be soppy, Dear," she said.

Marcia's put-downs of her husband were spoken with a fond tolerance, far removed from the scythe edge she used on outsiders like Sorah and me.

Luke stood up and walked to the front door.

"Thorvald's not going to attack us," said Matt.

Luke turned around. "What makes you so sure?"

"He always defended his own land. He never went off it to get at anyone. He wasn't armed when Kyle saw him down by the lake, and I'd guess he wasn't tonight. Isn't that right?" he asked me.

"Not as far as I could see."

"You can't predict the actions of a psychopath," said Luke.

"When did you become an expert on psychopaths?"

"Going to operas," said Marcia.

Even Luke laughed and then asked if we'd like a drink. Getting affirmative responses, he went to mix them.

Marcia asked if I were making any progress on her assignment, and I told her there didn't seem to be a chance in hell I'd find anything useful. It was plain that Sorah had come to the lake intending to capture P.J., she accomplished it, made him extremely satisfied with himself, and if

80

she killed him it was with something like kindness.

She stared at me, then looked at Matt and finally her husband. They looked back blankly.

"So," she said. "I gather the men are all agreed. If she loved him to death it was all a man could ask for, right?"

"What had P.J. been doing the day he died?" I asked.

"According to Estelle," said Matt, "he got up around six, his usual hour, ate an orange, took coffee in a thermos along with a bunch of red seedless grapes and some Farmer cheese and went fishing. He stayed on the lake until about nine-thirty, came home, had some more coffee with Sorah while she ate breakfast, and then they went into town for shopping. They had lunch and got back to the lake well before dinner, and he made some phone calls and hassled his broker. Estelle served prime ribs, baked potatoes, a mixed salad and apple pie à la mode. They had burgundy with dinner. We all joined them for a poker session starting around eight. He won some and lost a little; they went upstairs about ten. Less than an hour later, Sorah came running down to tell us she'd called a doctor but thought P.J. was dead."

"How'd she act?"

"Stunned, but in control," said Matt. "She didn't cry, Estelle told me, until the body was taken away. That was a little after midnight, I think."

"Did you see her the next day?"

"As far as I know, no one did but Estelle. Just went up to her room and stayed there. Estelle tried to make her eat, but she only took coffee and some toast."

"How'd Estelle take your questions?"

He said all right. She made it plain she felt loyal to Sorah, and he carefully avoided giving any hint he was looking for signs of foul play. The doctor had assured him there were no reasons to doubt it was a natural death. Marcia obviously felt there was nothing natural about death due to overindulging in sexual activities late in life.

Matt and I walked back to his cabin along the dark path. I felt some uneasiness about the place being deserted so long, and when we found everything was fine, admitted my concern to him. He laughed and told he'd worried too, but not a lot.

"Quite a while ago," he said, "I made up my mind I was never going to become dependent on things. I don't buy valuable furniture, first edition books, fancy gadgets or table silver. Don't even keep pets. I like feeding birds and taming chipmunks so they'll eat out of my hand, but if I get a chance to travel or decide to go camping, I don't want a damned thing holding me back. Sure, if anything happened to the cabin I'd be unhappy, but wouldn't be emotionally crippled or wail about irreplaceable treasures. I don't even keep photograph albums or boxes of pictures."

I respected his practicality but thought it was awfully sad to spend one's life avoiding vulnerabilities. When I got back to Minneapolis, I decided, I'd buy a camera and start recording people and places I wanted to keep.

Chapter 12

Light flashes jerked me awake and tense, until I heard thunder rumbling in the distance and realized it was only lightning. I rolled over cozily and was almost asleep when the wind came in a high rush; a tree cracked out front and toppled with a crash. Rain spattered against my window and began drumming on the roof.

I had a vision of Thorvald, huddled on the straw in his shed with a filthy blanket around him and a leaky roof overhead. The wind sounded strong enough to flatten his shelter.

Dazzling light filled the room again, the sky ripped open, thunder crashed and rain poured from the cabin eaves like a waterfall. I rolled out of the bunk, slipped into my moccasins and groped my way out to the front room. Another lightning flash, not quite so close, turned the downpour into a silver curtain beyond the windows and then everything was black again.

"My God," said Matt from his doorway, "poor Thorvald. If he hasn't found shelter he's gonna drown."

"If this keeps up, we all will."

We watched the lightning without talking as thunder battered the earth. In a few minutes it moved off, the rain slackened and we were able to make out the shining lake in erratic light from the retreating storm.

As usual, when a storm passes quickly, I felt a sense of letdown, but it evidently relieved Matt.

"Looks like we'll survive after all," he said. "Want some orange juice?"

I did and we went into the neighboring room where I sat at the table near the kitchen, and Matt opened the refrigerator. I saw its light and after a moment's fumbling he muttered something, rustled about, opened and closed a cabinet door and the refrigerator light went out. He came to the table carrying a plastic jug and two glasses.

"The fridge was raided while we were socializing tonight," he told me.

"What's missing?"

"The ham, a couple oranges, half a gallon of milk and a loaf of whole wheat bread."

"I guess you don't think any of the family did it."

"No, and it wasn't mice."

"Maybe Thorvald's collecting for the chickens he says Patsy killed."

He didn't get that until I explained what Peg had reported about her conversation with Thorvald when she went to his place and paid off his fine.

That was all news to Matt. He shook his head and said that was Peg all over.

"Just like her not mentioning the fact to anybody but P.J."

I expected him to ask me more about my relationship with his sister, but as soon as he finished his orange juice he said he was going back to bed. I guessed that meant he either didn't want to know more, or he thought I was such a straight arrow there was no concern. It also occurred to me I was being paranoid about the family's concern over Peg and me because the feelings she inspired weren't exactly brotherly.

I read and slept a little before rising at dawn, used the bathroom and took a cold shower. The only water heater in the cabin was a storage tank on the roof, and it hadn't had a lot of sun overnight.

There was no damage visible when I made a tour of the Krueger cabins and the white house. When I got back to Matt's, he was frying bacon and cooking something red in a pan.

"Huevos rancheros," he told me.

"No thanks. I had them in Mexico and my mouth's still sore."

"These you'll like. They use Tabasco sauce; I use one little red pepper and lots of tomatoes, sweet green peppers and onions. You'll love it. I also use toast, not tortillas."

He was right. I liked it mucho.

While mopping it up I asked if he ever locked the cabin during the summer. He didn't unless he was going to be gone for more than a day.

"Luke thinks I'm nuts, but I figure if anybody wants in, they can beat the locks with a crowbar or a rock through the window. I'd rather they walked in than broke in. P.J., Luke and Burt put up heavy shutters in the fall, and P.J. would like to have booby-trapped the place. So would Burt. It's funny, how they never liked each other but thought so much alike. They both went nuts over the fact a burglar sued and collected from a home owner who had set up a shotgun to go off when anybody tried breaking in."

I had to admit I felt people who committed murders and break-ins forfeited civil rights, but couldn't see myself killing anyone to prevent a robbery. To prevent or even avenge vandalism? Maybe. And certainly in cases of rape, the ultimate vandalism.

We cleaned up the kitchen and set off to see how Sorah was doing with her new boarders.

Jerry, the black-sheep brother, and his girlfriend, Phyl, were pulling duffle bags from the back of a four-wheel drive Toyota just as we approached the house. He was short and wiry with black curly hair and a wide grin that made him look like a handsome monkey. He had no resemblance to any of his siblings, and I couldn't help wondering if the total alienation from P.J. came from the father's suspicion this was not really from his sperm.

Phyl was fair, slim and a fraction taller than her mate. She embraced Sorah with great and unashamed affection, and greeted Matt with quiet reserve and a formal handshake. I got a cool nod when Sorah introduced me, but Jerry shook hands with both of us warmly, and I could tell Matt was very pleased to see him.

We went into the house, found Estelle at the sink and Ann Rose and Handy in the kitchen both drinking coffee. Ann Rose was wearing her gray slacks, pink sweater and a demurely shy face. Handy, in blue-jean cutoffs and a gray sweatshirt, rose to accept Phyl's quick embrace and a handshake from Jerry, who greeted Estelle and got snubbed. That only broadened his grin.

Estelle served coffee while Sorah explained to Matt that she'd decided death was the total forgiver (she didn't glance Estelle's way, but the message was clear) and she'd invited Jerry and Phyl as her friends and hoped the family would accept Jerry as a member for this occasion. Matt agreed it was appropriate, and we sat around the table on the back sunporch, chatting a while before Matt brought up the raid on his larder the night before. The Thorvald phenomenon was covered in some detail, and finally Matt said he thought we should tell the rest of the family about the latest.

That done, we left.

I asked Matt if Sorah's inviting Jerry came as a surprise to him.

"Hardly. Phyl's her best friend. They brought her together with P.J. and, above all, this is sort of laying it on the line that Marcia's not the queen bee around here."

"How will the others react?"

"Luke will have to be stand-offish because of Marcia, but he and Jerry never had any real problems so he'll be cool. Peg'll be tickled. She's always been sympathetic toward Jerry. I'd guess Burt'll be neutral."

Sandra met us on the path to her house and asked when people would be water skiing. Matt suggested after lunch and told her that Sorah had guests she ought to go see. She took off on a dead run.

"She's been stuck on Phyl ever since they went for walks last month and Phyl told her all about bugs. Next to skiing, Sandra likes bugs best."

"Why do you think Thorvald left the headless fish on Luke's dock?" I asked. "If he has to steal food, wouldn't he eat the fish and leave the head instead?"

"That'd be normal—but our boy's not exactly in that class. Besides, he probably lives on fish, figured the body'd be more noticeable and spooky. But we don't really know he's the one who did it. His only real gripe was against P.J., and I can't quite picture him as a terrorist. I mean, the raid on my refrigerator was strictly for sustenance; I can't believe it was a warning or even a threat."

It didn't seem too likely to me either, and I decided it wasn't something I was going to worry about much.

Chapter 13

We found Marcia in her living room thumbing through a *House & Garden Magazine*. Billy was on the floor, building a wooden block tower with the concentration of a chess genius.

"Did I hear a car pull up to the white house?" she asked.

Matt confirmed that and told her who.

"Great. Now aren't they a perfect pair to attend a memorial service? I suppose he'll get drunk—or is he already?"

Matt said he was fine.

She glanced at me and shook her head. "He writes dirty books for a living. And his girlfriend paid her way through nursing school modeling in the nude. Jerry met her while taking an oil painting class."

I said I didn't know he was an artist, and she said he wasn't. He took the course to meet models and learn about their lives, thinking it'd inspire him in the pornographic arts.

Matt asked where Luke was, and she said he'd gone fishing with Burt.

"You notice," Marcia told me, "that Matt's defensive about his little brother."

"Listen," said Matt, "we think Thorvald's alive and hanging around. Be sure to keep things locked up."

"For heaven's sake, why don't you call the police?"

Matt shook his head. "I don't believe he's dangerous, and I'd like a chance to talk to him before anything drastic's done. All he ever tried to do was protect his territory. That doesn't make him a homicidal maniac."

"What about murdering Patsy and shooting at the hunters?"

"Patsy was a dog in his chicken yard, and the hunters were trespassers on posted ground. I don't believe that damned story about him grazing Lundquist's hat. That son-of-a-bitch's always been a liar and I know he's poached deer and suspect it was him or his brats that vandalized Thorvald's place."

"So why does he haunt us? Why doesn't he go after them?"

"I don't know; maybe he has. Did you know Peg talked with Thorvald after he killed Patsy?"

Marcia looked incredulous.

"She told Kyle about it. She also paid the fine they hung on Thorvald."

"That's Peg," said Marcia. "All heart and no sense."

"Well," said Matt, "yesterday somebody raided my place for food. He didn't take much or do any damage, but you'd better keep your place locked up when you're out."

"Matt, are you crazy too? You've got to call the police! It's irresponsible to let an escaped lunatic run loose—and it's certainly doing him no favor. If he starts raiding cabins, somebody'll get hurt. Lundquist would shoot him on sight."

"Okay," Matt raised his hands in resignation. "I'll go to the county seat and talk with Rasmussen. See what he thinks. But first we'll tell Peg what's up."

Peg was sitting on the dock with her sons, Ted and Jimmy, and told us she'd been giving casting lessons. Ted had done fine until he got a backlash and wasn't too gracious about untangling it. Peg told him a true fisherman had to know how to untangle a line, so he sat on the dock and doggedly picked at it. His little brother watched and managed not to smirk.

"Can we bum some coffee?" asked Matt.

"You can even have a doughnut, if you're brave," she said. She reached for my hand and I pulled her up.

Inside, Matt told his tale of Thorvald's raid and Marcia's reaction.

"Don't turn him in," she said. "Let's go over there. See if we can talk to him."

"All right . . ."

"We could stake him, couldn't we?" she asked. "Get some supplies, some seed, a few chickens. If we can make him believe somebody really wants to help, maybe he can manage."

Matt said he'd give it a go.

"Let's do it now," said Peg. "I'll tell the boys I'm going to the store with you, and we can drive over to the shack."

I kept my misgivings to myself. Peg was so pitifully eager and earnest, any opposition would be cruel. A few moments later we were in Matt's Scout, jouncing toward the county road. After some discussion they decided to leave the car a ways from the gate and walk.

"Let me go first," said Peg. "We don't want him to think we're sneaking up on him. You guys wait by the road, okay?"

As usual, Matt agreed.

There was no sign of life when we arrived at the gate. For a moment we stood staring across the devastation, which looked sadder than ever drenched with the night's rainfall. The sun was bright, the air humid and the wind still. We could hear robins in the nearby woods and three crows flapped overhead, commenting in harsh caws.

Peg, who had brought a blanket and a bag full of home-made cookies, began walking toward the ruined farmhouse, clutching her peace offerings. When she was about fifteen feet from it, she called Thorvald's name. Only a distant crow answered.

She walked even with the farmhouse, stared at it a moment, then moved toward the machine shed. Twice more she called, then halted a dozen paces from the shed entry, identified herself and reminded him she was his friend.

He appeared in the dark opening so abruptly it made both of us start, but Peg showed no alarm.

"I want to talk with you, Thorvald, okay?"

Watching from the distance, standing in the bright sun, we could barely see him in shadows under the big black hat with a broad brim. I had an impression of close-set, deep-socketed eyes staring over Peg's head at us, full of suspicion and hate.

Peg took a step forward and he shrank back.

"I brought you a blanket and some cookies I made. Will you let me help you?"

He scowled at the offerings as she began walking slowly toward him. She didn't stop until she was close enough to hand over the blanket and cookie bag. He shoved the blanket under his elbow, and gripped the sack.

Peg began speaking too low for us to hear. He scowled at us again and asked a question. She answered quickly.

"I don't like this," I told Matt.

"Don't worry. Peg could soothe a shark. My God, he looks like a zombie . . ."

I remembered how swiftly he could move. Crows began making a racket off to the south, and Thorvald glared a them, curling his lip in a silent snarl.

A car came over a small rise to the east behind us, and we both glanced its way. When I looked back at the shed, Peg stood alone, staring into the blank opening.

We drove back to Matt's cabin in silence, and Peg remained quiet when we went inside until Matt persuaded her to tell us her impressions.

"I'm not sure. He's all wiry and hate-filled, but I felt no threat, or acceptance either. I didn't expect him to thank me for the stuff I brought, but it seemed like he could've shown interest when I offered help. He treated me like I was some stupid woman who didn't know what she was doing. It made me mad as hell and I suppose it showed. Maybe that's why he just went back in when the car came along and wouldn't come out again."

"You did fine," Matt assured her. "Don't expect miracles. You never tamed an animal in one afternoon, and you can't turn Thorvald into a pussycat in half an hour. Not even with your great cookies."

She shook her head sadly. "I should have given him money. Say it was to pay for the chickens Patsy killed. But I had a feeling he'd think money was insulting, like a bribe. Maybe he felt what I brought was that."

She stood and looked at a hummingbird glistening in the shaft of light that struck the red feeder a few feet from the window.

"Do me a favor," she said, without turning, "don't mention any of this to Burt, okay? Or anyone else."

She turned to face Matt. "Everyone but us feels threatened. They'd rather see him thrown in jail or driven away or even worse. I can't stand that. I think we hurt him. I know P.J. did. I just can't ignore that."

Matt told her he'd promised Marcia he'd talk to Rasmussen about the matter. "She assumes Rasmussen is a cop, but actually he's a psychologist who had a session with Thorvald before the judge decided to commit Thorvald instead of putting him in prison. I'll see what he says."

"Don't tell him we know Thorvald's around. He might have to report it to the police."

I asked Peg if I could use her phone for a credit call and she said of course.

"I'll go down to the dock so you'll have privacy," she said, "and Matt will go talk with Dr. Rasmussen."

A moment later I had the house to myself.

Edgar Hewitt answered his own phone, which was just one of the reasons he'd been my favorite resource in the charities field during my stint as a research reporter for a TV station. The other reason included his long experience in fundraising, his critical mind and sharply analytical views.

We exchanged polite talk about recent activities before I asked if he'd mind giving me his impressions of a colleague.

He asked who and I said, "Burt Beattie."

He laughed. "I'd think you had him pretty well pegged after he jumped all over you for the charities fraud special you ran."

"I'm seeing him in a family setting and have learned another side, but I need something more."

He wanted to probe that, but I avoided details. He said I hadn't changed a bit; it was all get and no give. But okay.

"He's a professional with maybe a tad too much ambition. Having it's okay; showing it isn't. You know about the legal suit he got into a while back?"

I didn't.

"A rich woman donor he'd been cultivating died and left him a bundle. Half a million. The family sued, claiming undue influence or the like. It got lots of attention in our business. You can't imagine what intimacies develop between donors and really good fundraisers. I'm not talking hanky-panky here; it's something different. Donors tell us things about themselves they'd never mention to their families. I'm not talking scandal, but dreams and weaknesses. What changes they'd like to make in the world, how they'd most like to be remembered."

"How'd the suit turn out?"

"Oh, Burt came out fine. Proved he hadn't been in touch with the woman for over five years before she died. But it caused such a to-do he turned the money over to the University Foundation for medical research. You might say it was an investment in his career."

"Last question," I said. "What happens to a body turned over to the University for research? They do an autopsy?"

"It goes into cold storage until they schedule it for study. Could be months. I'm not sure of the procedures from then on, but it's not likely anyone does any examination looking for unnatural causes of death—which I assume is what you're getting at."

"You're warm. Thanks a lot. I'll be seeing you."

"Uh-huh. If the killer doesn't get to you first."

Chapter 14

After my phone call I found Peg gazing at her two sons in the rowboat near the shore east of Matt's cabin. She had shed her white cover-up, revealing a black and white one-piece swimsuit that bared her hips nearly to the waist, but almost covered her beautifully rounded bottom. It was a remarkable job of engineering, and she caught me admiring the result.

"I suppose I'm getting a bit old for this sort of thing," she said, looking down at herself, "but compared with what Sorah and Ann Rose wear, I feel Victorian."

I assured her that at twenty-nine she was far short of ancient and lucky to be living in more enlightened times. She considered that a second, smiled warmly and suggested I come up to the cabin and help her start lunch.

She asked me to make peanut butter and jelly sandwiches for her boys, and she prepared tuna fish salad ones for us. We'd drink tea, she said. I asked if she was expecting Burt to eat with us and she shrugged.

While I cleaned the radishes, she asked if I believed she was unrealistic about Thorvald.

"Probably."

"You think he hates people, don't you? That he lives on the edge and is really dangerous?"

"He's demonstrated it."

She smoothed the already flat tablecloth with graceful hands and frowned.

"Estelle's daughter rode the same bus with Thorvald when they went to grade school. She says he was very quiet and shy. Never had serious trouble with other boys and talked only when she started the conversation. He worked for his father on the farm he lives on now, only then there was a nice barn and a normal farmhouse. His father was the old-time religion type who thought having fun was sinful. I don't think Thorvald got to sin much. His mother was odd, maybe retarded. She treated him like a puppy, but was afraid to be too affectionate because the old man thought that'd spoil him."

"What happened to the house and barn?"

"They were wrecked by a tornado that killed his mother, crippled the old man and just wiped them out. Thorvald was about seventeen, maybe less. He dropped out of school to care for his father and the farm. The father died within six months. Some of the neighbors, including Estelle's family, tried to help out, but he didn't know how to thank folks or show appreciation, so naturally they quit trying eventually. And then, when he got nasty toward kids playing on his land, he became the county pariah. Things like that build fast in a rural community."

The boys came in for lunch, and Peg fed them but suggested she and I wait to see if Matt might return and join us.

When the kids were through, she sent them off again, warning them to stick close to the dock.

At one o'clock she decided the heck with Matt, and we sat down to our sandwiches and tea.

I asked how Burt's problems with the lawsuit had affected the family.

"It raised hell."

She went into little detail, but obviously the experience had revealed character flaws in Burt she'd never seen before. When the suit began he'd been enraged, overly defensive and obnoxiously righteous. Her suggestion, early on, that he turn the money over to the University Hospital research fund had made him so mad he'd stalked out of the house and not shown up again for three days. When he came home, he told Peg she was right, and he was going to follow her advice. But he made no apologies for his rage or temporary desertion.

"He hated me for being right," she said. "It got him in very well with the University people, of course, that's why he finally made the decision. I think it took him the three days to swallow the fact a half a million dollars wouldn't make him a millionaire. And then he was terrified about having people think he'd suckered a senile old woman."

"How is he as a father?"

The question seemed to pain her. Finally she said he had his good moments, but the big troubles were inconsistency and, except in front of guests, indifference.

"He liked them best when they were totally dependent. As each hit the terrible twos he gave them up. Jimmy still seems to have hopes that he's loved, but Ted pretends he just doesn't care whether Burt notices him or not."

"What are you going to do?"

She fiddled with her cup, took a deep breath and sighed.

"I suppose I may as well go the whole hog and tell you what's going on. I've picked a successor to Burt. Don't get nervous, it's not you. Do you know Gregory Talbott?"

I didn't.

"He's a lawyer who worked for P.J. in the late eighties and came around to our house a lot when I was still in high school. We got innocently involved while I was at the U. Right after I married Burt, Greg married a fluff-head who left him for some wild musician. I called Greg six months ago to discuss divorcing Burt. One thing's led to another al-

though not all the way yet. I'm old-fashioned and he's understanding, so it's not been too bad. He's sold on the boys,
not having had any kids of his own, and they've seen
enough of him to think he's great."

"Does Burt know what's going on?"

"I'm not sure. He's so self-centered he doesn't notice
much, but on the other hand he's not stupid. I've noticed
lately he's been working at being nicer to the boys, and I'm
nasty enough at this stage to suspect his motives."

We were on third cups of tea and out of sandwiches
when Matt came in. He asked where Burt was, and Peg said
he was fishing with Luke and she didn't expect him until
late afternoon.

"Now don't be coy," she said, getting up to make him a
sandwich, "what'd Rasmussen say?"

Matt took a chair, accepted tea and leaned on the table.

"He says Thorvald's anti-social but a long way from dangerous unless crowded. Just wants to be left alone. Rasmussen also explained the death story. The guy killed was
named Foster. He was built like Thorvald and wore the
same kind of clothes, so one of the dazed survivors mis-
identified him. They assumed the guy who wandered off
was Foster because he'd pulled the disappearing act twice
before, and after a couple days they'd located him in Iowa.
When they got the bodies straight, no one worried because
Thorvald had been passive the last year. Rasmussen agreed
he wouldn't blow a whistle on him being back around here
as long as he doesn't cause any problems. I promised to report anything weird and said I'd check in on him now and
then."

"Did you tell him about the fish on the dock?" I asked.

"No. We don't know Thorvald did that. I don't want to
complicate things with stuff we only suspect."

"You think maybe somebody else is trying to make us think he's a thief and threat?"

"I wouldn't put it past Lundquist or his brats."

When Matt finished eating, we left Peg and wandered along the beach path to P.J.'s dock where Sorah was stretched out on a canvas lounger adding to her tan and talking with Jimmy. Ted was practicing dives off the dock.

"Where's Handy?" Matt asked her.

"He and Ann Rose went into town. He's meeting a sporting equipment man who figures Handy'd made a great demonstrator. I suppose Ann Rose wants to do some shopping."

Sandra and Billy came around, and before long Matt had been coaxed into taking the kids skiing. The three boys got to ride in the boat while Sandra had first turn on the skis. I sat beside Sorah, watching.

"I think we should talk," said Sorah.

"Fine."

"Phyl tells me she lied to you about whose idea it was for me to come out here the first time. I've told her you were bound to know better from Matt. She was just being loyal. I didn't put her up to it."

"Did you meet P.J. at the clinic?"

"Yes."

"What kind of treatment did he get there?"

"He got a prescription that's administered with a syringe in the penis."

"I'd think that process would pretty much shoot romance."

"Well, it's not exactly foreplay. P.J. would go into the bathroom and take care of it before joining me. Evidently he thought it was worth it."

I didn't doubt that a hell of a lot of men would, even if

99

the needle was big enough for a horse doctor's trade.

"So he kept the medication in his bathroom?"

"No. It was in the bureau beside the bed."

"Who knew about this business?"

"I suspect everyone in the family. Jerry got it from Phyl, he undoubtedly told Matt because it was the sort of thing he'd think was enormously funny, and I imagine Matt told Luke because they're very close."

"Would you mind showing me the bedroom?"

She gave me a thoughtful stare. "You're taking your assignment seriously, aren't you?"

"I think I should. I'm grateful you're taking it so well."

We went through the spacious living room, climbed the curving stairway and walked past the expansive bedrooms until the last on the southwest corner. The old man had been overfond of white, and most of the house had a hospital sterility that left me cold. The bedroom was different. There were large, bright abstract paintings on three walls. Windows lined the south overlooking tall pines and small maples covering the slope beyond. I edged up to one of the more garish paintings and read the signature: J. Krueger.

I looked at Sorah, who smiled in amusement.

"These are by Jerry, the black sheep?" I asked.

"Yes. I told P.J. I wanted some color and he said fine, and when I put them up he acknowledged they brightened the room. He never looked at the signature when I was around, but I suspect he did on his own and figured I was pulling a trick on him. Of course I never let on. He was an incredibly aware man and very tolerant about me. I had hopes, back then, that I could make him tolerant toward Jerry. I should've worked harder at it sooner, but I'd no idea how little time I had . . ."

The drawer where P.J. kept his erector set was part of an elaborate headboard with an enormous mirror and flanking cabinets. Sorah opened the lower drawer, lifted a small cardboard box from under a sweater and handed it to me. She rummaged a second more and came up with a plastic-wrapped syringe.

I opened the box, removed a tiny bottle labeled Papaverine Hydrochloride. Its plastic top flipped off easily, revealing a metal cover and under that the opening exposed a tannish, rubbery material.

"You insert the needle into that," said Sorah, "and fill it by pulling back the plunger."

I tried unscrewing the metal cap but it was clamped on.

"If someone wanted to substitute something poisonous for this stuff, it'd have to be done with a syringe, right?"

"I guess so."

I examined the label again and found "poison" in red letters on a green background.

"That's not too reassuring," I said.

"It's just a warning to use as directed."

I read the printed directions, which included information about contraindications, precautions and adverse reactions. The only encouraging note was under "Drug abuse and dependence." It assured the patient that no cumulative effects had been noted following use of papaverine, which had a low toxicity and no record of tolerance and habituations caused by administration.

Practically like aspirin, only with a needle.

I asked, "Why would he go through all that when there's Viagra?"

"He was scared of it. He knew someone who had a bad reaction. Then he read reports of two deaths and wouldn't try it."

"Well," I said, "thank you. This has been very educational."

"From your reaction," she said, "I think you've learned more than you wanted to know. Shall we go back to the beach?"

Chapter 15

Sunday evening Handy joined Matt and me for dinner and while we ate pan fish, boiled potatoes and corn on the cob, he described his visit with the exercise equipment manufacturer. The man had been friendly and enthusiastic, and the product literature impressed Handy, who had already seen and even used some of the gadgets. He guessed he'd start work next month.

It was plain he wasn't excited about his prospects, and I wasn't sure whether his low spirits came from Ann Rose's indifference to the whole program or her decision to have dinner with Sorah instead of us.

Matt asked what was going on at the white house. Handy said the two women were talking a lot.

"Ann Rose and Sorah seem to have become instant old buddies," I said.

His face betrayed a flicker of concern before he controlled it. Then he said it was probably because they both felt like outsiders among the Kruegers and their longtime buddies.

"What do they talk about?" asked Matt.

"When I left it was art. Sorah'd shown Ann Rose Jerry's paintings in the bedroom and some other stuff he'd let her have, and they were going on about it all. Sorah thinks Jerry's a tragic case."

"Marcia told me Jerry wasn't a painter," I said. "You think she just hates abstractions?"

Handy looked at me thoughtfully but kept quiet as Matt explained that Marcia didn't figure any painter was real if he didn't make a living at it or hadn't been dead for half a century.

"Jerry's prolific as hell," Matt went on, "and he's not just into abstractions. He's done a mess of nudes that're nearly photographic."

"Maybe pornographic?" I suggested.

"It probably started that way. But what he does now has no eroticism at all. They look more like expensive manikins than women. The flesh tones seem perfect, but when you look at them a while there's no warm body under the surface. It's more like enamel than skin and it's deliberate. I don't understand why."

"Maybe that's what women are to him," said Handy after a drink of water. "I don't think he likes women much. The dirty books are full of dummies. There're no real women there."

My eyes must have popped a little. I'd assumed he'd consider pornography as unhealthy as red meat. He caught my stare and ignored it.

"What about Phyl?" asked Matt. "She's sure no dummy."

"She's more like a partner than his woman. He likes her, I'm sure, but—"

We heard footsteps coming up the path to our door, and the next moment Jerry tapped and came in.

"Greetings, primitives," he said, "I come bearing an invitation. Sister Peg called the white house and wants men in her cabin. It seems she's been deserted by her hubby."

He laughed when we gaped at him.

"Okay, I exaggerate. But Burt's wandered off with Luke, and Peg wants to talk and is afraid to leave her boys alone because of the prowling mad farmer. So she called Sorah, and I've been sent to fetch you guys."

Matt thanked him, said we'd go over, and turned to Handy.

"Mind watching the place while we're gone?"

"No problem."

"I'll keep him company," said Jerry. "The women up yonder won't let me talk anyway."

The sun had sunk just below the wooded slope. Matt set a rapid pace as we headed for Peg's cabin along the lake shore. There was no wind and its glossy surface reflected a clear sky and the north star.

Peg greeted us at the door with apologies which Matt waved off.

"Burt and Luke are up to something they don't want me to know about," she said. "That makes me think it involves Thorvald. Luke's afraid for Sandra and Bill, and Burt's been acting weird ever since the fish business. I think they're going to do something stupid. They were gone all day, supposedly fishing, but when Burt got home his boots were dusty so he's been somewhere besides the lake. After eating dinner he said he was going back to Luke's cabin. They've never been this cozy before. I thought I heard a car leave, and when I called Marcia, she said they'd gone to town. Claims she doesn't know why and thought I was being nosy. She didn't say as much, but she always lets you know when she's disapproving. I don't know why I let her bug me so, but one of these days I'm going to let her know how I feel about it."

Matt's attempt to be soothing only irritated her. I suggested that he and I drift over to Thorvald's place and look around.

"Oh," said Peg, brightening, "would you?" She reached across the table and touched my hand. "I'd be ever so grateful!"

Matt wasn't that pleased but agreed, and we went out the back way and stood a moment, discussing whether to drive or walk. We decided to walk.

It was turning darker, and the north star was brighter than before and gaining company.

"I'm not convinced this is smart," Matt said. "Luke's not the kind of man who's going to do something stupid. If he's as shook as Peg thinks, he might go raise some hell with whoever he blames for letting Thorvald run loose, but that'd be it. I'm afraid our barging into Thorvald's territory might just stir him up again."

"We don't have to barge in," I said. "We'll just take a look."

"The real trouble," he admitted, "is I'm worried about Peg. She's not herself these days. I just don't buy this business of Burt fooling around, not after his grief from that lawsuit. I mean, he's got to be extra careful about image and reputation right now. This is a guy who takes pride in being a professional. He dotes on approval, admiration, respect, all that stuff. I can't believe he'd lose his head over a woman, especially Sorah."

"Do you believe he over-promoted himself to the woman donor?" I asked.

"Oh sure. He just didn't realize how far she'd go."

I wasn't convinced. He might have thought she'd leave him several million, in which case I didn't believe for a second he'd have handed it over to the U. or anybody else.

We swung around to Matt's cabin so he could pick up a flashlight, and told Jerry and Handy where we were headed. Handy wanted to come along, but Matt persuaded him to stay in the cabin.

"We aren't going to get in trouble—this is just to ease Peg's mind."

106

We went out and were just starting toward Thorvald's farm when we saw Sorah running toward us.

"There's a fire!" she cried. "We can see flames out the back window—it looks as if it's coming from Thorvald's farm!"

Chapter 16

We arrived before the volunteer firemen and saw the ruined cabin and machine shed ablaze and heard it crackling. Other neighbors were looking on, all strangers to me. One chunky man drifted over beside Matt and nodded curtly. His thick glasses reflected the flames and hid his eyes. A thatch of graying hair covered his forehead, almost meeting the bushy eyebrows, and his wide mouth sagged slightly, exposing stained teeth.

"Thorvald," he said, watching the flames.

"What?" asked Matt.

"Thorvald done it. He's loose, y'know."

"Oh, you've seen him?"

"Kenny did. Caught him raiding our apples and run him off. Let him know what he'd get if he come back."

"How come you didn't call the cops?"

"We can watch out for our own."

"You called them when you said he took a shot at you."

He grinned briefly. "He had a gun then. Cops took it away from him. I ain't afraid of his hatchet."

As we drifted away, I asked if that was Lundquist.

"Yeah. Joe. Kenny's his older son."

We found Jerry and Handy playing checkers back in Matt's cabin. After our report, Jerry conceded the game to Handy and hurried off to join the women in the white house.

"Why do you think Lundquist said Thorvald burned his own place?" I asked Matt.

"Probably because he or his son Kenny actually did it."

"You don't think it could have been Burt and Luke?"

The idea startled him at first, and then he shook his head violently, but I felt it worried him as he thought of it. I suggested we go see if Luke and Burt were home. He shook his head again.

"No, it's too late. We'll deal with it tomorrow. Right now I'm going to bed."

After Matt retired, Handy rummaged in the refrigerator and came up with a glass of cranberry juice. I poured a small cointreau. When he'd finished his juice he casually walked near Matt's bedroom door, then strolled toward the kitchen exit.

"Going for a walk or just to take a leak?" I asked.

He paused, filling the doorway. "Both."

"If you're going to look around, I'd like to come along."

"All right."

After he'd stopped at the privy we walked the path along the lake and checked on each of the cabins and the white house. There was still light in the latter, but the cabins were dark and silent. We circled them, then walked toward the farm. Handy moved soundlessly in his soft moccasins. By contrast my steps echoed in the night.

The farm was deserted. The volunteer firefighters had drenched the charred remains of the shack and shed, leaving nothing but the sad stench of ruin. Crickets sawed away, an owl hooted and we heard a distant cat yowling in ecstasy or rage.

"You think Lundquist could be right?" I asked. "That Thorvald set the fires?"

"That's bull."

"You think it was Luke and Burt?"

He took a deep breath and let it out slowly. "If Marcia told them to, yeah."

"Why'd she—?"

"She seems like a tiger about family. Maybe if she got the notion he might hurt any of them, she'd see he never got the chance."

Such thinking would be about as rational as her hiring me to prove Sorah had murdered P.J. And then I began wondering what motives Marcia might have for killing P.J. It could be jealousy, outrage or even sheer frustration. She was probably the only member of the family angry enough about Sorah to orchestrate a murder, and she was certainly cunning enough.

But these were idle thoughts. I didn't believe she was cold-blooded to that extent any more than I could convince myself that P.J. died of anything but natural, if exotic, causes.

Something caught Handy's eye in a row of elms south of the burned buildings, and he began a circuitous approach, very slowly. I went along. When we were within yards of the first tree on the east end of the row, Thorvald's lean figure moved swiftly from behind a center tree and darted west.

"Damn," muttered Handy as we halted and watched the wraith disappear in the nearby woods.

"Well," I said, "at least we know he's still alive."

"Yeah, you could call it that."

We walked to where Thorvald had stood behind the tree and stared around.

"What are you looking for?" I asked.

"I don't know."

After a moment we started back toward the gate.

"What would you have done if you'd caught him?" I asked.

"I didn't expect to catch him. If he'd stood still I'd have tried to talk with him."

"About what?"

"Anything. Just see if he could be reached."

"Peg couldn't manage, and she's done a lot of things for him."

"Yeah. It was probably stupid. But I'm not one of P.J.'s family and I'm a man. It might make a difference to a guy like him. He's probably scared of women."

"I think a guy your size'd scare him more than any woman."

He conceded that in silence, and when we reached a parting point he faced me.

"You sleep light, don't you?"

I admitted so.

"We both better. I'll keep an eye on the white house and cabins. You watch out for Matt."

"You think Thorvald is going to try something?"

"I'd bet on it like a royal flush."

I wished him good-night. He nodded his clipped head and glided away.

In Matt's cabin I sat in the easy chair in the big living room and thought until the frogs stopped croaking, birds began to sing and the lake began turning silver with dawn.

Chapter 17

At breakfast I asked Matt if Burt actually turned over his inheritance to the University Foundation.

"Every dime."

"That must've been tough. Peg says he worries about being able to send the boys to college."

"Well, that's a stylish reason to give for wanting a bundle these days. The truth is, spending most of your working hours with people who're loaded can't help giving a man big ideas about status and advantages. Burt's a guy who needs status and loves advantages."

"Have you ever noticed him coming on to Sorah?"

"Let's say he's deferential. But then, that's how he treats all people with money, so it doesn't make him exactly suspect."

The catering crew was already at work on the lawn in front of the white house when Matt and I walked over a little after nine. Two men were setting up a three-sided yellow and blue tent. Matt stopped to talk with a squatty character he called Ed, a guy he'd known in high school. Ed told me he always figured Matt was the kind who'd stay in school all his life. "And," he concluded, "he probably figured I'd be swinging a sledge all mine."

"A rustic wit," Matt told me as we moved along. "His old man owns the catering company, but he always plays the poor hired hand. Loves calluses. He wanted to be a pro baseball player, but couldn't hit a curve."

"You seem to know all about everybody you've ever met," I said.

"Wish I did."

Handy was at the table with Marcia and Luke when we entered the kitchen. His face showed lack of sleep and something else I finally decided was discouragement.

Luke admitted he and Burt had given up their fishing the afternoon before and set off intending to catch Thorvald and turn him over to the authorities. He wasn't defensive about it. He said when they drove through the farm gate, Thorvald popped out of the machine shed and took off for the woods.

"We never touched him or even spoke to him," said Luke. "After dinner we went into town and talked with Jonas in the sheriff's office, and he sent a couple men out to look around. He's convinced as we are that Thorvald shouldn't be running loose."

"No one in his right mind would think differently," said Marcia, looking at Matt.

"What do you think he'll do now his shelter's burned?" Matt asked his brother.

"He could move in with Sorah," said Marcia. "She's accepting all comers."

I thought Luke winced, but he kept his mouth shut.

"Who set the fire at Thorvald's farm?" I asked.

All eyes turned on me in varying stages of disapproval. It was evident that subject had been silently banned by the family.

Marcia finally responded. "Who do you think?"

"I don't think it was Thorvald."

"I do," she said. "He realized everyone knew where he was hiding so it was dangerous to stay. He burned it to throw suspicion on us and get sympathy for himself."

"It was all the home he'd ever had," I said.

"It'd been defiled, ruined beyond recovery. It'd be quite natural for him to complete the destruction."

113

"What do you think he'll do next?"

"Come around stealing food, like a rat, 'til somebody catches him and puts him back in a cage."

"I hope that's the worst that can happen," said Matt.

Luke stirred and looked at his brother.

"You think he'll be after revenge?"

"I wouldn't have, before the fire," said Matt. "All along I've said the only thing Thorvald tried to do was protect his own. Now he's got nothing left to protect—and he knows people from here've been coming around to his land. Who else would he blame? What's he got left but rage?"

Marcia got up and began clearing the table.

"You're forgetting something," said Luke. "You say he never did anything but protect his own. What about that warning he left on my dock? The headless northern?"

"That was a warning, not an attack. Besides, we don't have any evidence that he did it."

I agreed in silence. It was too subtle a threat for a man like Thorvald.

"What about your neighbor, Joe Lundquist?" I asked. "Maybe he set the fire."

Matt liked that idea. It gave him a great deal of relief. "Of course. He was there when we went over, all dressed. And it's just the kind of thing he or one of his sons'd do—"

Marcia agreed instantly. Handy's face stayed blank and Luke only looked at his wife. After a little more talk, Matt and I left.

The tent shelter was complete as we approached the white house, and two men were setting up a long table for the buffet. Sorah was talking with Ed, the squatty man, who nodded at us and wandered off as we approached. She wore a crisp, trim and rich white summer dress and smiled at us radiantly. A silk scarf splashed with black and gold caressed her slender neck and a larger scarf in a matching pattern made a belt around her slim waist.

"Isn't it a wonderful day?" she said. "It never rains on the Fourth of July!"

"It's not over yet," said Matt.

"We're going to have white sangria," she told us. "It's a little like champagne, you can drink it with anything."

"White sangria," I said, "sounds like an oxymoron."

She laughed. "That's exactly what Jerry said. He also denies it's good with everything, but it is with all I intend to eat."

She had evidently pushed the events of the night before from her mind, or more likely they were crowded out by preparations for the party, which was beginning to look more and more like a wedding reception than a simple family gathering.

Matt asked for the party program and Sorah assured him it was strictly casual. The sangria would be served about one o'clock, when there'd be small snacks, appetizers and salads. Later there'd be barbecued beans, sweet and sour meat balls, potato salad of two kinds, raw vegetables with onion and clam dips, and finally rock Cornish hens roasted on a spit over the charcoal burner and basted with a special mix of rosemary and oils.

"After dark, we'll have a fireworks display, for children of all ages."

"You sure there'll be enough to eat?" asked Matt.

She laughed. "I guess I'd better tell you of a little surprise I planned. Some of P.J.'s closest business friends are coming. A very select few, ones he really liked, and to be honest, ones that accepted me. I felt they were the ones who appreciated him and should be considered like family."

Matt stared a second before asking who they'd be.

"Geoffrey Ashland, Olin Stensrud and Mac MacGlothlin."

"And their wives?"

"Olin and Mac will bring theirs. Geoffrey's a widower. He may be bringing a lady friend. At least I urged him to. You don't mind, do you, that I've invited them?"

"Of course not, it was very thoughtful . . ."

"And Burt'll be happy, don't you think?" There was a clearly impish look on her face, and it made Matt smile.

"I don't think he'll be offended. His big problem will be deciding who to concentrate on."

"I'm sure it'll work out smoothly. Now maybe you can help me with a problem. How can I keep the sangria cool in the big crock we're using, without putting in so much ice the drink'll be diluted?"

"I'll just fill a plastic bag with ice cubes, tie it up tight and stick it in the crock."

Sorah was delighted and while he went to work on that, I drifted over to Burt's dock and found Ted and Jimmy paddling in the nearby water, wearing water goggles and looking for fish. Ted told me they hadn't found anything but minnows and perch.

He kept looking, but Jimmy was bored and climbed up on the dock to sit by me.

"Aunt Sorah's gonna have fireworkers tonight," he informed me.

"She told you all about it, huh?"

He nodded. "There's gonna be a guy over on the point there," he pointed, "setting stuff up. Rockets and bombs and all kind stuff. Aunt Sorah's rich."

"You like her?"

"Uh-huh. We're gonna have cake 'n ice cream too."

116

"Sounds like a great party. Did you know your grandpa well?"

He looked doubtful.

"Did he ever talk to you?"

"He said, 'Wipe your feet' when we came up from the beach and 'Wipe your mouth' when we ate."

"You go to his house much?"

He shook his head.

I asked if his Aunt Sorah told him to wipe his feet and mouth and he said no. "She always says, 'Have fun.' "

I felt a step on the dock behind me and glanced around to see Peg approaching. She was in her swimsuit and a swimming cap that made her head seem small and her face large.

"Are you grilling my son?" she asked.

"Do I know you?" I responded.

She laughed and touched the swimming cap. "I know, it makes me look like a pinhead but I don't want to get my hair wet before this afternoon's bash."

"You look fine. It makes your eyes bigger than ever."

"Don't flirt with me, Kyle, I'm very vulnerable to you."

"You look dauntless. I take it P.J. didn't dote on his grandchildren."

"He mostly ignored the boys and pretended to tolerate Sandra, but actually she fascinated him. You want to swim over to the point with me?"

I said yes. At the cabin I always wore swim trunks for underwear so it was a simple matter to peel down and join her in the water. Ted wanted to come along but she told him it was too far and we'd be back soon. He pretended he didn't care and went back to looking for fish.

After we dove I came up slightly beyond Peg and took off, knowing her skill. Without exertion she caught up and

117

plowed by. I dug in. She was sitting on the beach grinning at me when I splashed up beside her and grabbed for her foot.

"What're you doing?" She laughed as she tried to pull away.

"I wanted to see if your toes were webbed," I said, letting her go.

"You nut. I could beat you when I was fourteen, but I never did because I thought you'd hate me for it. Now I have more respect for your maturity."

"But no concern for my male vanity. Can you beat Burt?"

"I can beat anybody but Matt. Sometimes I think he's got a motor up his rear—which you always claimed back in those days."

I stood up and looked at where a man was working on a platform of three wooden pallets lined along the bank above the water. It was Ed, the caterer's son.

"You do everything, don't you?" I said to him.

"I don't swim much."

"You going to set them off tonight?"

"Nope. I'm not willing to work twelve hours on the Fourth. Burt'll set 'em off according to a schedule I'll leave with him."

"I guess Sorah arranged all of that, huh?"

"You mean Mrs. Krueger?"

"Yeah, that's her. Mrs. P.J. Krueger."

He grinned. "She's quite something, ain't she?"

Yes, I agreed, she certainly was.

Chapter 18

Peg and I lazed our way back to the dock, and after we had sun dried a while she suggested the boys go up and have a banana apiece to hold them until the buffet opened at P.J.'s house.

Ted told her it was Sorah's house now. She agreed he was right, but said since P.J. had built it, she'd always think of it as his. That got her a what-can-you-expect-from-a-woman look before her macho son took off for the cabin with Jimmy trailing.

She watched them, smiling, and shook her head.

"I guess you can tell Ted's not exactly crushed by his grandfather's passing. Like all the other males in this clan, he thinks now he can have Sorah to himself."

She glanced at me, frowning.

"You still don't really believe that Burt's involved with someone, do you?"

"Well, I haven't seen or heard anything, except from you, that'd make me think so, no."

"You maybe don't even believe he's unfaithful, do you? You think because I'm interested in another fellow I've worked up this idea of him messing around to make it okay for me."

"I don't think you're that simple."

Her smile looked sad. "Thanks. How long did it take you to know when your love life had gone sour?"

I shrugged.

"Come on," she said, "don't give me that. You're sensitive enough to have caught on the minute it started. You might not have admitted it even to yourself, but sensitive people can't miss the signs, and you and I are sensitive. We watch and know people we're close to. I'm not going into the details of how I know Burt's turned off. Just take my word for it, I know. It's not just the usual thing of a husband losing the excitement. The truth is, Burt's never been exactly a sex maniac, and he's not affectionate enough to compensate. I hate how I sound, I don't want to be like this, but I'm beginning to hate him for what he's making me into. He's up to something. He swings between treating me like a dowager queen and not knowing I'm in the same room with him, let alone bed. I'll admit I had silly notions of what marriage would be like—the last thing I wanted was what I saw between my mom and dad. Well, this is sure as hell different, but worse. P.J. cared about what Mom thought of him; Burt only cares about what the *world* thinks of *him*. He's got this ego that needs feeding and what I offer doesn't do. Whatever weaknesses Burt has, he's not foolish enough to think being with rich and powerful people all the time makes him one of them. So he has to get his satisfaction out of working them for all he can and does it well enough to satisfy himself that he's smarter than they are. He's always looking for the worshipful eye, or some way to make himself important to people with power."

She pulled off the tight swimming cap, fluffed her hair and stood up.

"Enough. I've got to go slip into something less comfortable and prepare for the day. I'll see you at the buffet."

Since Sorah had decreed the uniform of the day was strictly casual, Matt and I put on knit shirts, shorts and deck shoes a little before one and strolled over to the white house.

We found Estelle working the spigot on the sangria crock

and as she spooned a thin slice of apple into my glass I couldn't resist asking if she ever had a day off . She told me coolly that she had chosen to share in the memorial for Mr. Krueger in her own way. Jerry, who had received his potion ahead of me, muttered, *"belle sentiment!"*

Jerry joined Matt and me in canvas chairs under a trimmed weeping willow near the buffet tent. Jerry looked disreputable as usual in floppy red shorts and an oversized T-shirt imprinted with a tipsy golden gopher on the front.

"Where's Phyl?" Matt asked Jerry.

"Helping Sorah and Ann Rose fix stuff for the buffet. Handy, believe it or not, is delicately cutting up raw veggies. Somehow, although the face is no match, I keep picturing him as the closet gay bodyguard played by a guy in that movie with the English canary and James Garner."

As he spoke, the trio appeared carrying loaded platters. Sorah was all high fashion in a white jumpsuit that made the most of her slim waist and long legs. She wore a black silk kerchief around her neck, I assumed as a token of mourning, but to offset the potential gloom, her sandals were decorated with miniature roses where straps crossed above her toes. Phyl's outfit looked like something to play tennis in. Handy's navy blue slacks, pale blue short-sleeved shirt and black shoes made him look relatively formal.

When Sorah had arranged the platters on the buffet table, she came over to ask how we liked the sangria.

"It's perfect," Jerry assured her. "Tastes like fruit juice and carries the kick of a mule."

"I got the recipe from a Spanish bartender when P.J. took me from London to the Costa del Sol for a weekend. The secret is extra brandy, go heavy on the wine and light on the soda, plus lots of fruit to camouflage it all."

"Secret of a great party," said Jerry. "Get 'em drunk

early, feed 'em late. Everybody thinks the food's great no matter what they get and they pass out early."

"The food," said Phyl, "is sensational, so don't you dare get smashed before you try it."

He said yes, mother, and she cuffed him on the shoulder.

By half past one all the family was present and generally scattered among tables set up on the lawn with canvas chairs. The buffet was under attack and the kids were well into it with pop from a cooler at one end of the big table under the tent. Sandra wanted to know if this big party meant there'd be no water skiing, and Burt told her sententiously that her grandfather had hated the sound of power motors so there'd be none of that, and she should show some respect.

Peg looked at me and rolled her eyes.

Geoffrey Ashland made his appearance at two. He didn't have much going for him other than exceptional height, lush wavy hair white as fresh snow, the face of an aristocrat, the smile of a TV star and a bony frame that carried tailor-made clothes as casually as common folk wear jeans and T-shirts. He greeted the family members, including the kids, by their first names, had a word for each, identified Handy and even remembered where he'd played high school football, and told me with a straight face that he missed seeing me on TV since I left it. His most impressive show of class was the restraint when he spoke with Sorah. He treated her like a bereaved daughter without overdoing it and told her P.J. would have been proud of her today.

She responded with a demure smile, a brief handshake and said she'd be needing investment advice from him in the near future.

I thought I detected a flicker of embarrassment as he glanced beyond Sorah at the family members within hearing. He was sensitive enough to look for their reactions to the reality of this young woman being the millionaire's solely named heir. And for a moment I wondered if Marcia had been right, that Sorah did intend to rub in their losses.

Sorah led him to the sangria and asked lightly why he hadn't brought a friend as she'd suggested. He said it didn't seem appropriate since no one he was keeping company with these days had known P.J.

"Then you're seeing young women?"

He laughed and said yes, P.J. had set an example that made all his old friends either envious or imitative.

"Being single," he added, "I'm able to take the happier route, however risky."

He watched her closely following that remark and was relieved, I thought, to see her smile.

Sorah introduced Jerry as P.J.'s younger son whom he'd never met, and told him this was the artist who'd painted the pictures displayed in her bedroom. Geoffrey showed keen interest and asked if he had much work on hand. Jerry, for the first time since I'd met him, looked flustered while Phyl hastened to assure the man there were a number of works available for sale.

I'd been taking this in from a position near the sangria crock and suddenly found Marcia at my elbow.

"See how she operates," she murmured, nodding toward Sorah. "She's already given the stockbroker a clear invitation to get in touch with her, has introduced him to her indigent brother-in-law so he can do her a favor by becoming a patron of her buddy and all the while puts the rest of us in our place, on the sidelines."

Without waiting for my response, she asked if I'd been

123

able to find out how Sorah restored P.J.'s potency.

"A doctor did it," I said.

"Medication?"

I nodded.

"So, there you have the means."

"Marcia, the means to kill are infinite to any wife."

"Oh yes, but it's infinitely better if self-administered, right?"

"Any member of this family had access to his medicine cabinet, including you."

"Not with her ease. It'd be very tricky, as a matter of fact, to avoid the danger of being caught. Besides, what motive would I, or any of us, have?"

"Rage. Revenge. Jealousy. A few others."

She stared at me. "You're suggesting that all the men wanted access to that woman. That's what you're saying, isn't it?"

"I'm saying that all of you, including the women, had motives as valid as Sorah's."

"That's nonsense. If Peg or I were going to hate, it'd be directed at her, not P.J. And none of the men are stupid enough to kill him thinking they'd be able to win the widow."

"The widow had no pressing need to become single when she had a doting husband who was certain to die while she was still young and desirable."

"I see. So he died a natural death, and we don't need a private detective, we need a good lawyer. Obviously that's the next step."

I wished her good luck with what I hoped would pass for sincerity. If I fooled her, she hid it well.

Chapter 19

Olin Stensrud and his wife, Echo, arrived in a Mercedes sedan not long after Geoffrey had settled in. Olin looked oriental with his slanting eyes, gold complexion and straight black hair. His thin-lipped smile showed priceless teeth. Echo wore a broad-brimmed straw hat, sunglasses, and a black-and-white summer dress which covered her from neck to ankles but didn't conceal that she was over-breasted and under-hipped.

She grasped Sorah's hands when they greeted each other, kissed her on the cheek and murmured what I assumed were condolences, but for all I could hear she might have been telling her she looked terrific in mourning.

After a pause at the sangria crock, Sorah brought them around for greetings and introductions. Echo's mouth, except for artfully applied lipstick, matched her husband's, right down to the perfect small teeth which appeared in a smile so mechanical I expected to hear it click when she acknowledged me.

The only people they made any pretense of knowing or remembering were Marcia, Luke and Burt. Echo leaned over Marcia, once more murmuring sympathy or its equivalent, and Olin gave Luke the old fellow-clubman's double handshake.

Burt played the complete professional. He waited until they came around to him—I'd expected him to dash up the instant their car appeared—and shook hands with a fine balance of respect and warmth.

Overall, the Stensruds conducted themselves like British

royalty being gracious to the little people.

Geoffrey came up from the dock where he'd been with Sandra and Ted, and greeted the newcomers familiarly. The two children, while disappointed by the distraction, responded to introductions with proper courtesy.

Echo told Sorah she'd like to go inside and freshen up, and they went toward the house while Geoffrey, Olin and Burt settled under an umbrella at a round table. I assumed they were discussing money.

"What's Olin do?" I asked Matt.

"It's not what, but who, and I'd say taxpayers, mostly."

He explained that he was with a major manufacturing company specializing in government contracts.

"He and P.J. go back to the Korean War days—that's when they made it big together."

A few minutes later Sorah rejoined the party. I drifted up to the house and walked through the living room on my way to the main floor bathroom. Echo was sitting in one corner of a large couch facing the windows, exposing a pale, sloe-eyed, hollow-cheeked face faintly reminiscent of Marlene Dietrich.

Her smile came on less mechanically this time, but still fell shy of warm. I nodded, passed on through, used the bathroom and came back to pause beside her.

"Allergic to sun, or just the company?" I asked.

She put down the magazine, examined me thoughtfully for a moment and said, "Would you get me a drink? And I don't mean that sugared and fruited crate wine in the crock."

"What'd you like?"

"Scotch and water. Easy on the water and never mind ice."

I went to the bar, found Chivas Regal and a moment

later handed her a lowball glass with what she'd ordered.

She took a drink and tipped her head toward the space beside her. I sat down.

She turned, facing me more directly, and frowned.

"You look oddly familiar. Like someone I've seen in a news story or a magazine article. I'm afraid I didn't get your name."

I told her.

She shook her head and I felt I was offending her by not being familiar.

"What do you do?"

"Lately I've been a private detective."

"Really? One of those security people? Insurance?"

"Murder."

Her highness was not amused. She looked down at the magazine she'd dropped in her lap when I handed over the drink, and for a moment I thought I was going to be dismissed. Then she looked at me again.

"How well did you know P.J.?"

"Very casually. I come into this scene because I used to stay here often during the summers when Matt and I were college classmates. Played poker with the old man a couple times."

"And lost, I presume."

"Mostly."

"P.J. was always a winner. Except with his family. You know he couldn't stand his first wife?"

"I heard there were differences."

"If that's all you were aware of, you must be a lousy detective. He despised the woman. It even overlapped onto the offspring because they liked her best. P.J. couldn't play second fiddler to God. Is Estelle still around?"

"She's serving the sangria."

"No kidding. Old anonymous Estelle. She was his mistress once. Did you miss that too? Well, it was a long time ago. But she always knew who number one was. I'm surprised she didn't slash her wrists when he died."

"She's working on this holiday to honor his memory," I said.

"How noble. I see Marcia has her grief under control."

"Don't tell me—"

She laughed. It was harsh and filled with delight. "Yes indeed, P.J. had her too. The only woman in the family he missed was Peg, and I wouldn't bet on that."

I didn't ask her about Matt's wife.

She handed me her empty glass, and I went back to the bar and filled it.

"In case you're wondering," she said as I handed her the drink, "no, he never made out with me. He didn't even try very hard. He wasn't interested in women who could see through him."

"I didn't think he was that good-looking."

"Looks in real men don't mean a damned thing. Not to real women. It's the style, the power the man radiates. Men like Picasso, Onassis, and Gates. Not Greek gods, by any stretch, but they could have any woman they chose."

I thought perhaps she was bitter because P.J. hadn't tried hard enough for her.

She drank with satisfaction, cradled the glass in her lap and focused on me again.

"Did you really go to the U. with Matt, or is that your cover for a job here?"

"We met in a writing class during our freshman year."

She watched me over the rim of her glass while taking another drink, then nodded abruptly.

"So you're a private detective who deals in murder. Very

interesting. Now I remember. You were involved with the foundation director murder, the one-time banker, Fletcher. He was killed in Mexico—"

"Uh-huh."

"You wouldn't think, by any chance, there was something a tad neat about P.J.'s departure from this world so promptly and conveniently after changing his will?"

"I'm just vacationing here."

"Sure," she said, "and I'm Mother Teresa."

Chapter 20

I was mixing Echo's third drink when I heard someone entering the kitchen and looked in to see an amply-padded woman in a floor-length cover-up directing a younger woman to the kitchen counter where she put down a cardboard box and began opening the top.

"Happy Fourth," said the padded lady, giving me a dimpled smile. "Who're you?"

I told her and she said oh yes, but the vagueness in her gray eyes belied the assurance in her tone. She took a tall, red warming pot from her companion and plugged it into a wall socket.

"I figured Sorah'd have lots of the usual snacking crap and brought a couple specialties to liven things up. Wakes call for lots of livening up. Is Geoffrey here yet?"

"Everyone's here but the MacGlothlins, so I guess you're Corliss."

She flashed me a smile with enough warmth to supply Echo for a week and introduced me to Pamela, her nubile daughter who was still taking things out of the carton.

"Pamela's at loose ends because she just dumped her boyfriend and couldn't snare a replacement this late."

"Mother," said Pamela with a note of exhausted patience, "don't start laying out my whole personal life to a perfect stranger."

"I doubt he's perfect," said Corliss, giving me a measuring look, "but you could do worse. He looks like he might have some sense, and God knows that'd be a lovely change for you."

Pamela's eyes, which as far as I knew had taken in nothing but the contents of the carton and some consideration of the ceiling after her mother's crack, said I was too old for her.

"Much," I agreed.

That got me my first direct look from the daughter.

"After P.J.'s choice of Sorah," said Corliss, "I'm about convinced age makes no difference."

"Yeah?" said Pamela. "And look what happened to him."

"So he died happy and Sorah's rich. Who lost?"

"The rest of the family."

"There speaks a girl who hopes to be an heiress," Corliss informed me.

Echo appeared at my elbow.

"I'd appreciate it, dear," she said to Corliss, "if you wouldn't distract my bartender. I'm about to expire."

"You do look awfully faint," Corliss agreed. "Go on, Kyle, fix her up."

A little later I stood beside the barbecue pit where Luke was skewering rock Cornish hens on a long, silvery spit after stuffing each with an onion. He shoved them together in obscene intimacy and screwed the prongs tight. The coals were already glowing and spread neatly around a trough of aluminum foil placed to catch falling fat and juice.

I noticed Sorah, Corliss and Echo in conference under a green umbrella at a nearby table and caught occasional glances my way, which suggested they were discussing my role at the party. The rich men sat at a table nearer the lake and I saw MacGlothlin sitting with his broad back to me, and a huge dog at his side.

Pamela had overcome her aversion to my seniority and

lingered near, not, I was sure, because she found me fasci-
nating, but because I was the only single male present and,
even in my advanced years, closer to her age than most
present.

I asked where she went to school, and she said Bryn
Mawr and made it clear she wasn't going to talk about
courses studied or her social life there.

"Is it all that bad?"

"It's all anyone wants me to talk about and I'm sick of
that."

"You interested in politics?" I asked.

"Yuck," she said.

"Movies?"

That topic was okay but ran dry when we found that
Anna and the King and *The Red Violin* were the only shows
we'd both seen recently and there was no disagreement
about their high quality.

She told me after a while she thought it was pretty sick
to hold a drinking party in celebration of a man dying.

"Most of us don't think of it as a celebration," I said.

She giggled.

"What's funny?" I asked.

"You are."

"How so?"

"You've missed the whole point of all this. It is a celebration. Nobody's really sorry he's gone. He was a lech-
erous, self-centered old bastard."

"Ah, did he make a pass at you?"

"He never had a chance. Before Sorah I was too young
and after her he never had time. He tried everybody else,
though. Talk to my mom. She can tell you."

It took a while. I found her back in the kitchen after I'd
made another bathroom visit. She smiled her warming best

and said she hoped I hadn't had trouble eluding her daughter.

"You caught her with that crack suggesting she was too young for you. Nothing attracts her more than a man who's not interested. If you want to get rid of her, just make a pass."

"She's very attractive. I suppose she gets bored with the constant rush."

"Yes, fortunately she doesn't take after either of her parents. Looks just like my older sister who was the family beauty."

"She tells me P.J. was a letch."

"Really? What an odd subject to come up at a wake."

"I got the same impression from Echo."

"Are you really working for Marcia?" she asked. Her tone suggested disappointment.

"Is that the story going around?"

"There doesn't seem to be much question about it. Okay, P.J. was a womanizer, or liked to fancy himself one until Sorah came along. His first wife was a very frustrating woman for a man like him. She couldn't take him seriously, and it drove him frantic. If anything calls for investigation around here, I'd say it'd be her death. No man wanted freedom from a woman more than he did from her."

"Do you know P.J.'s sons very well?" I asked.

"Oh sure. Since they were tads. Especially Matt. I never saw much of Jerry, who was a rascal from the cradle, but I've talked with Matt lots of times. He's a very understanding, intelligent man. I almost said boy. It's hard not to keep thinking of him that way."

"You know what broke up his marriage?"

"Who ever knows? I've never believed that sort of thing is ever simple."

"It wasn't anything like his wife getting involved with P.J. then?"

She stared at me. "Where in the world did you get that idea?"

"It seems to fit what I've been hearing ever since I got here."

"I don't think that's the sort of thing you should be talking about. Particularly today. Did Pamela tell you something?"

"Does she have something to tell?"

"I don't think I want to talk with you any more. I will tell you that Sorah told both of us to be absolutely open with you, and I'm trying, but I really don't like the way you're going about things. It's insidious. I don't think you're a very nice man. I won't tell Pamela that because it'd only make her more interested, but I wish you'd leave her alone. She's young and highly vulnerable to suggestion. I don't want you perverting her thoughts."

I assured her I would avoid all suggestiveness and said I was sorry she was offended.

She waved her hand and went upstairs. I returned to the front yard. Pamela moved toward me from the sangria crock.

"Well, did you talk with Mom?"

"I did."

She grinned at me. "What was the reaction?"

"She's disappointed in me."

"Oh yeah, that's one of her best moves. I guess you didn't ask her if she'd slept with him. Then she'd really have gotten mad. Are you really a private eye?"

"I don't have a license, no."

"You're just sort of a freelance snooper, huh? Matt says you used to be a TV news reporter and even an anchor man for a while. Isn't the private snooping kind of a come down?"

"I'm trying to rise above it. How about you introduce me to your father and his long-haired friend?"

She agreed and we went over to the table where he sat with Geoffrey, Olin Stensrud and Burt. The huge dog turned his long head and gave me a crocodile grin. I was surprised to see a collie's muzzle on the bear-like body.

MacGlothlin was compact as an oak stump with curly reddish gray hair thinning at the top. A white, short-sleeved polo shirt exposed brawny red forearms a tattooist would love; his mug was sunburned raw. Bushy eyebrows, with wild tufts he obviously wouldn't let a barber touch, gave him a comedic expression, which fit the story he was telling about the man who was going to apply for his social security. The man's wife told her husband he should take his birth certificate along to prove his eligibility. He said he'd lost it, but wouldn't have any trouble, and she told him he'd get nowhere. A few hours later he came back looking smug. She asked how he'd managed to get by without proof, and he said he's simply unbuttoned his shirt and showed the gray hairs on his chest.

"Well," Mac concluded for the wife, "you should've unbuttoned your pants and showed them why you ought to get disability pay too."

When Pamela touched his shoulder, he turned and grinned up at her.

"This is Kyle Champion," she said. "He wanted to meet you."

His small, watery blue eyes peered at me through the tufted brows.

"I don't give autographs," he said.

"That's okay, I don't accept them."

He chuckled cozily and patted the dog.

"This is Jesse. Short for Jesse Ventura. Pam wanted to call him that because he's the greatest. Shake," he told the dog. It raised it's right paw and I shook it.

"Jesse'll be staying with us a few days," said Burt. "The MacGlothlins are going to Switzerland and Luke's looking after him."

"Nice timing," I said.

Burt gave me a bland smile, but his smugness made me think he'd managed the arrangement.

MacGlothlin placed his empty sangria glass on the redwood table, stood and pulled his pants up.

"Let's take Jesse for a walk," he said.

"Why not?" I agreed, and we started down toward the dock.

Chapter 21

"You know what Marcia's problem is?" asked MacGlothlin.

"Her mother-in-law's young enough to be her daughter."

His grin displayed fewer teeth than his dog did, but it was still quite a display.

"That's part of it," he granted as we began walking out on the dock. "But the real problem is, she was too close to P.J. Marcia's never been a good loser. Smart as she is, like most women, she lets her head take a backseat when the problems slip below the waist. You follow me?"

"This is only a woman's problem?"

He ignored that and went on.

"Doc Elliot says P.J. died of myocardial infarction. That's medicalese for heart attack, likely caused by overexertion. Said there was no call for an autopsy. Now unless you figure Doc Elliot was bought by somebody, you've got a perfectly natural, not to mention ideal, death. You going to second guess him because a jealous woman's trying to make it murder? You need money that bad?"

"Nobody's paid me a dime. My old friend invited me for a long weekend, and his sister-in-law asked me to look things over and see what I thought. That's all there is to it."

He reached down, rubbed his dog's furry head and patted his shoulder.

"I hear you're writing a book about Better Business Bureaus," he said, examining his dog's fur.

"Where'd you hear that?"

"Probably in news stories about you nailing Fletcher's

137

murderer. I read 'em because I knew Fletcher back when he was my favorite banker. You got a contract for this book?"

"Have to finish the outline first."

"Ah, but you've been too busy. I wouldn't think there's much future in the private eye business."

"Could be."

"Now in television, who knows how far you could go?"

"I already found out."

"Nah. Just in news. Take commercials. There's real money there. And lots of other jobs if you've got the right connections."

"You know them?"

"You bet," he said comfortably.

"When would I start?"

"Like tomorrow."

"I wouldn't be free that soon."

"Too bad," he said, and stopped petting Jesse. "I guess you got tired of TV?"

"It went a little both ways."

"Yeah. Well, like Rambo said, 'A man gotta do what he gotta do,' right?"

"That was Rocky."

"Whoever. One thing's sure. You won't have much of a future in the snoop business."

"Who's going to see to that? The same guys that could give me a commercial career?"

He shook his head. "You got quite an imagination. What you ought to do is write fiction. That's a job for a man like you."

We went back to the party, and if there was any signal passed between the millionaires, I missed it.

I looked for Matt but he was busy talking with Luke, and then I met Peg returning from a quick plunge in the lake.

"I think I've just been leaned on," I told her.

"By Mac?"

I nodded. "He knows Marcia wants me to check out your dad's death and claims it's because she's jealous. Sexually."

"You mean he thinks Sorah was fooling around with Luke?"

"No. More like Marcia and P.J. were cozy."

She stopped in the path, took off her swimming cap and squinted against the bright sun as she looked up at me.

"That's ridiculous."

"Maybe. But I got the same line from Echo. And Mac suggested if I was willing to start tomorrow, I'd have a new future in TV."

She glanced over my shoulder toward people at the tables around the barbecue and then met my eyes again.

"Did you say you'd think it over?"

"I said I'd be busy."

"You're crazy." She said that severely, then flashed her impish smile. "But I love it. What'd he say'd happen if you kept poking?"

"That I wouldn't have much of a future."

Her smile vanished as she looked past me again. "Oh dear."

"You know something about Mac that I should hear?"

"No, not really . . . but since you don't believe Sorah killed Dad, wouldn't it be a lot easier to just go along with him?"

I admitted that made sense and wondered why neither of us took the idea seriously.

Sangria flowed and most people ate almost as steadily as they drank except Echo, who eventually lurched down from the house and got embarrassingly interested in Handy's remarkable physique. Stensrud, who I guess had lots of practice, eased her away from the athlete, thanked Sorah for inviting them and hosting such a splendid wake, and hustled off.

The departure of the MacGlothlins got more complicated. When Mac wanted to leave, his daughter Pamela objected, saying the party was just starting. Sorah suggested she stay on, assuring her parents that she'd be given a ride back to the Twin Cities within a day or two—whenever she preferred. Corliss said maybe it was a good idea, since they were leaving the dog and it would help to have a family member still around for at least the first night. Mac at first objected, then abruptly agreed and they left.

There was an elaborate ritual of taking Jesse into the house and feeding him while the MacGlothlins quietly made their getaway. Matt, who did the feeding, told me later the dog obviously knew what was going on, ate indifferently and, at the moment the car started, pricked up his ears, rushed to the door and gave one long wail. Matt tried to comfort him, coaxed him back to the food dish and felt quite proud that Jesse seemed to accept matters rather quickly.

Geoffrey lingered, managing most of the time to be near Sorah without being too obvious. While he always had a glass of sangria in hand or close by, it was never more or less than half full. Sorah drank just enough to keep an even, happy glow.

By late afternoon Handy had adopted Jesse and I saw them stroll off into the woods. Ann Rose stuck close to Sorah. Since Burt kept hovering around Geoffrey, they were practically a foursome. Soon Ann Rose, realizing Geoffrey was working on Sorah, set out to distract Burt. She asked how he kept in such wonderful condition and wished she could see him water ski again because he was so graceful and exciting on the skis. Before long he was explaining the techniques of riding a single ski, and when she begged for a demonstration he came over to our table and asked Matt to handle the boat. Matt put him off, and he irritably moved on to Luke who, after some discussion, agreed.

"So much for his respect-for-the-dead line," said Peg, who was sitting with us and watched them head for the dock.

The water skiing got expanded after Burt's exhibition, which ended when he took a cartwheeling fall that caused no serious visible damage but seemed to wound his psyche. Sandra coaxed Luke into taking her for a round, and the whole party stood on the dock, watching the child show up her uncle. She was inspired and, of course, had the advantage of total sobriety.

Eventually the skis were retired and the boat tied up. Matt suggested that he and I row over to the point and check out the fireworks.

"I thought Burt was going to run the display," I said.

"Burt's in a sulk and, if I know him, will probably sack out. I want to check the directions Ed left and see if I can handle it."

Pamela, who was still sticking close to me, asked to go along and was accepted.

Matt rowed while Pamela and I sat in the bow seat. Pamela was stripped down to a bikini in midafternoon, which left her wearing not much more than a gorgeous tan.

"I'd guess you swim a lot," Matt said.

"I sunbathe a lot," she replied.

"I've never understood how people can do that. Don't you get bored to death?"

"Nope, I read."

"What?"

"A. S. Byatt, Anita Brookner, Salinger, Dorothy Parker, short stories by Marian Thurm and Mary Gaitsksill—"

141

"These are just lately?"

"So far this summer."

That silenced Matt and made me a little thoughtful as we pulled up to the beach at the point. We climbed out and had just started up the beach when we heard something crashing through the brush toward us. We halted, then raced back to the boat, and as Matt and I each grabbed an oar, Jesse charged out of the brush and came to a skidding stop on the beach.

"Dammit, Jesse!" yelled Pamela. "You scared us about to death!"

Handy showed up seconds later, and the worry on his face showed more expression than he'd ever displayed before. He apologized to Pamela, saying when the dog took off he was certain he'd spotted Thorvald and was scared somebody'd been killed.

Pamela hugged the dog and laughed.

"He sounds like a charging rhino when he runs through the woods," she said. "I should've recognized it the moment I heard him. Isn't he gorgeous?"

"Looks like great minds run in the same channels," Matt remarked to Handy. "You figured you ought to check this out?"

"Yeah. We went over to the farm. Thought I'd just see if maybe the ghost was hanging out near there and figured Jesse'd find him, but we didn't stir up a thing. So I came around here."

Matt checked out the directions Ed had left with the fireworks setup and then asked Pamela if Jesse ever barked.

"I'm afraid so. When everybody's gone to bed he turns into a big-mouthed watchdog. Sounds off if a mouse breathes."

"Fine," said Matt. "That's just what we need."

Chapter 22

Back at the white house desserts had been spread on the long table under the tent. In addition to cake, ice cream and strawberries, Sorah offered an assortment of after-dinner drinks. I took Kahlua, Pamela had crème de menthe and, as we strolled down the slope, she asked what her father had wanted to talk about when he suggested we take a walk.

"Did he offer you a job?"

"It was more like advice. He suggested I get back into television."

"When we were driving up here he said something to Mother about a job for somebody that'd be here. I wasn't really listening, since I hadn't met you yet and didn't know anything. There was something about a private detective too—I was reading and didn't pick up on it. Were they talking about you?"

I said it was likely.

She stopped walking and sipped her drink while studying me

"Okay," she said, "there's something weird about P.J.'s death, right? So who's hired you?"

I decided there was no point in waltzing around my role again.

"You know which person here is Marcia?" I asked.

"Yeah, she's the queen bee of the hive. Married to Luke, the second oldest."

"Okay. She wanted me to check things out. That's what I'm trying to do."

Her eyes went from round to narrow as she leaned close.

"So. Marcia's green because Sorah wins the works, right?"

"You've got that straight."

"And Daddy thought you ought to find something else to do. Isn't that interesting? You're telling me he told you to lay off."

"Well, let's just say he made an interesting alternative offer."

She looked up toward the house and frowned. "He's great buddies with Geoffrey, and Geoff's hot for Sorah."

She leaned close. "So you're going back into television?"

"No."

She stared at me. Her blue eyes were enormous, and it wasn't all due to makeup, which added only emphasis.

"What'd he say when you turned him down?"

"He said he didn't see much future for me in detecting."

She shook her head. "You should have taken the job."

"You think I'm in trouble?"

"Honey, you're in deep shit, if you'll pardon my French. Real deep.'

While Estelle and the only remaining caterer carried the sangria crock up to the house, Sorah called the guests together at the tables on the lawn and gathered the children in a band at her feet.

"It's time for a little announcement," she said. "There's been a lot of concern, I'm sure, about how our small friends here will be able to go to college when the time comes. This was a concern of P.J.'s, even though he never said anything to you about it. I want you to know a trust fund's been set up to guarantee tuition and living expenses for all of P.J.'s grandchildren at any school they choose and qualify for."

I looked at Marcia whose face froze a second, then slowly produced a smile, more knowing than appreciative.

Peg glowed. Burt looked stunned. Luke nodded thoughtfully. The small boys weren't impressed; they were waiting for the fireworks to begin. Sandra managed to look pleased.

"So now we can get on with the fireworks," said Sorah, turning her smile on Burt.

"Are you telling us," asked Marcia, "that this was P.J.'s idea?"

"He didn't suggest this specific plan," she said. "I just know he'd approve. We never discussed his legacy. The only thought he ever had about dying was that he didn't want cremation, embalming, burial or fuss. He wanted things simple and trusted me to handle everything when he was gone."

"Flawless judgment to the end," said Marcia.

"I'm glad you see it that way. Burt?"

He got up, still looking stunned, and headed for his boat. Handy followed, taking Jesse with him. A moment later the motor roared to life, and they were streaking toward the point.

"Cheez," muttered Pam leaning close, "where'd she get the notion Luke and Burt are on welfare?"

"It's all relative," I muttered back. "These days putting a kid through college can bring you to that—God knows what it'll be in a dozen years."

We heard Burt turn off his motor and immediately Jesse was barking. Peg, who was sitting at the table nearest the shore with Pam, Jerry, Phyl and me, worried out loud that Thorvald might be hovering near.

I said I didn't think the man would dare face the dog.

"He certainly faced Patsy."

"She wasn't a collie, was she?" I asked.

"No . . ."

"I'd guess old Thorvald'd be more in danger than Jesse," said Jerry.

"That's no comfort to me," Peg told him.

The barking stopped after the fireworks began. It was a good show, lots of lovely color and sharp sound. Of course, it didn't last long enough to suit the kids, who knew they'd be herded off to bed as soon as it was over.

Matt asked Handy when they got back what Jesse had been barking at, and he said he didn't know. He'd charged into the woods barking the moment they landed, then came slinking back when the fireworks started. Pam said fireworks and thunder turned him chicken.

Handy patted the collie, which grinned shamelessly at us.

I saw Marcia herding her children home, and Peg decided she should get hers to bed too.

Phyl, I noticed, kept staring back up at the table nearer the house where Sorah and Geoffrey sat talking quietly.

"Looks like a budding romance," said Jerry, who'd begun drinking scotch and water after the meal.

Phyl gave him a dirty look. "Don't be stupid. They're talking investments. That's why she invited him in the first place—he wasn't all that big a buddy of P.J.'s."

"They sure make a knockout of a pair," said Pam. "I guess money's as good a topic for getting involved as most."

"And we know Sorah's vulnerable to rich seniors," said Jerry.

"I think you're a pig," Phyl told him. "Sorah's not a gold digger."

"You're out of date," he told her. "These days you call her type a pragmatist. Gold diggers went out with Busby Berkley movies in the thirties."

Ann Rose came down from the house, joined Sorah and

Geoffrey and a moment later Sorah laughed. Phyl turned abruptly toward Handy.

"Have you given up on your girlfriend?" she demanded.

He looked startled, and Jerry came to his rescue.

"You giving up on yours?" he asked.

"Don't be an ass," said Phyl, getting to her feet. "I need another drink."

There was an awkward silence as Phyl left and paused at the neighboring table. She spoke to Sorah, who nodded, got up and accompanied her to the house.

"What's going on?" Pam asked Jerry.

"The usual. Phyl's possessive of Sorah. Gets pissed when she comes up with new interests."

"Are you telling us she's jealous?"

"Naw, I wouldn't say a thing like that. She's just ambisextrous. No problem."

"Why'd P.J. get so sore at you?" I asked him.

"Everybody gets sore at me," he said. "It's the price of an over-developed sense of humor. That and I didn't appreciate him. Ran away. He said, fine, you don't like it here, don't try coming back, and we settled on that arrangement. I was fourteen at the time."

"Mother financed him," said Matt.

"Beyond all need," he said airily. "By the time I was sixteen I didn't need her help. The county took care of me."

"You were on relief?"

"Nope. In reform school. I was the youngest guy ever nailed for pimping in Minnesota. It was quite a distinction. Had three girls working for me when it was blown. Nice kids. One older than me."

"I think you're lying," said Pam.

"All right, she wasn't older than me by much. Just two months. I guess that doesn't really count."

"I guess," I said, "that P.J. knew about all of this?"

"Bet your ass. Sent him the clippings myself. In case he missed them. He didn't get much beyond the market section of the news. Anybody else want another drink? I'll buy."

Chapter 23

When mosquitoes started humming around the lawn, Sorah invited everyone inside and offered drinks or coffee to those interested. She asked Geoffrey to light the fireplace, which had been laid in advance, and stood watching her guests settle in while the fire crackled behind her.

"I thought it'd be nice," she said, "to end the evening by the fire, talking about P.J. and, since he hated conventional rituals, we couldn't have a funeral and put the final touches on his life in the usual way. Maybe this is cheating a little, but I think we need it and believe I knew him well enough to say he'd appreciate this need even though he never felt it himself."

Peg said that was a wonderful idea, but she was nervous about leaving the children alone in the cabin. Luke persuaded her that Jesse would raise the alarm if anyone came around, and Handy volunteered to patrol the area, so she was satisfied.

"Matt," said Sorah, as she settled into an easy chair, "you're the first son, why don't you start? Tell us your very first impression of P.J."

Matt stroked his goatee, frowned at the fire and for a moment seemed at a loss. When he spoke it was slowly, with pauses between each sentence.

"I was standing beside him in the kitchen of the first house I knew. His hip was level with the top of my head and he had his hand on my crown. It was heavy. I ducked and pulled away, and he laughed and said I was going to be independent, just like his dad. Later he carried me on his

149

shoulders. He taught me to duck as he passed through doorways and was irritated when I tried to grab his head. He thought I didn't trust him."

"He mentioned that to me," said Peg, "when I was only four or five. He couldn't stand it that you didn't trust him absolutely. Isn't it strange he'd have such a fixation?"

"No," blurted Jerry, "he always thought he was God almighty, and it was sacrilege to doubt him."

"What do you remember, Luke?" asked Sorah quickly.

"It's weird," he grinned faintly. "I remember him belting Matt for hitting me. I can still see Matt when he came into our room right after. His left cheek was red from the slap, and the expression on his face made me feel real sorry for him. I started to cry, and he got mad at me again, but he didn't hit me."

"I was never a slow learner," said Matt.

"How come," asked Jerry, "the old man never slapped Luke for hitting me?"

Luke gave him a tolerant smile. "You never dared tell on me because you always knew you had it coming."

"He'd have thought so, no matter the reason," said Jerry.

"What about you, Peg? What do you remember?"

"Oh, lots of things . . . Going fishing with him most, I guess. He took me because I didn't get bored or talk all the time like the boys. And he taught me how to swim, how to get over my fear of water, and he bought me a new fishing rod and reel when I won my first swimming race."

"Ah yes," said Jerry, "you were always Daddy's little girl. Until you got married and blew it—grew up and saw he wasn't God. Was that as tough on you as it was on him?"

"Jerry," said Sorah, "don't be like that." She turned to Geoffrey and asked if he'd describe his first meeting with P.J.

"Love to. He was the speaker at a Rotary meeting I went to right after the Korean War ended. He gave an inspirational talk. I was so excited by it, I went up to the podium afterward and introduced myself. Before I could say a word about how wonderful his talk was, he gave me the lift of my life. He said he'd been hearing great things about me, that I was a comer and how about we have lunch on Tuesday the following week at his club? I went and he introduced me to Stensrud and MacGlothlin and others, all great contacts. He was a genuine dynamo and the best friend a man could ask for. There'll never be another like him."

"Thank God," said Jerry softly.

Geoffrey turned toward Sorah and asked for her favorite memories.

"Oh no," she protested, "there's not enough night left and most of it's too personal. I'll just say amen to what you said. I was lucky to meet him when I did, I'm grateful for the time we shared, brief as it was, and I'll never forget him. And I want all of you to know how much I appreciate sharing this day with you. I know he hurt some of his family, and I'm deeply sorry about that and hope you can forgive him. I also hope you know I never deliberately did anything to cause problems between you and him."

"Nobody with sense ever thought you did," said Jerry, as he glared Marcia's way.

Sorah smiled her thanks, and at that moment the dog exploded in a frenzy of barking.

Marcia and Peg came to their feet and were joined by their husbands as they ran for the door. Matt and I followed them out, but stopped with Handy who was unhitching Jesse's leash from an iron stake. He said he'd just been coming back from Burt's cabin when Jesse began barking.

"Let's go," said Matt and they took off after the charging dog.

I considered going with them and rejected it. If Handy hung on to the leash, I didn't believe they'd ever catch the slippery Thorvald, but even if they did, I wasn't interested in being part of the hunt.

Sorah, followed by Geoffrey, stood a moment nearby until the hunters disappeared south in the woods. I saw him link his arm in hers.

Pam came up to me.

"I don't like this," she said. "I don't like any part of it."

"Will Jesse attack a man?" I asked.

She shook her head. "The only way he'd hurt anybody is to stumble over them."

"Then the chase probably won't come to anything. At best, they'll scare Thorvald off."

I looked around and saw Phyl standing just outside the front door, glaring at Sorah and her escort. Jerry, I guessed, was pouring another drink.

"What do you think that madman's trying to do?" asked Pam.

"Probably plans to torch one of the cabins."

She shuddered. "I'm sorry I asked. Which one?"

"The handiest. He figures all of us are against him, even though Peg tried to help. He'd probably like to fire this one most, but it's the hardest to get at because the land's all clear around so he couldn't sneak up easily. Matt's place is the most vulnerable. The trees and brush run right up to its walls."

The dog's barking was distant by now.

Pam tilted her head, sighed and said, "I guess I won't join you tonight."

I looked down at her. "Had you been planning on it?"

"It came to mind. Maybe you should come and stay in my room here. I wouldn't allow penetration, but I like to fool around. We'd have fun. I'd let you do lots of things."

"Aren't you afraid I'm kind of old for such excitement?"

"You're not old and besides, I'm sick of young guys. They're so dumb. Do people like anchormen have groupies? I mean, do you get lots of girls being on TV and all?"

"I was never that big an item and I've never gone much for quickies."

She gazed south where Jesse's bark had almost faded away. When she spoke again she didn't look at me. "I don't mess around with just anybody, but I really love being wanted bad. It's probably stupid . . ."

"I think it's pretty normal."

"If not common?" She looked up at me.

"You're not common by any stretch, but between us friends, I don't think this's a night for messing around."

"Are you playing hard to get because Mom told you I'd like that?"

I laughed. "I'm afraid I'm not that calculating, Pam. I hope that doesn't disillusion you."

"Okay. Walk me up to the house and kiss me good night. You can risk that, can't you?"

I thought I could and did. It was a nice kiss, one I might even be able to confess to Peg about, but not feel too guilty if I kept it a secret.

"How much longer are you staying at the lake?" she asked as we drew apart.

"Maybe a day or two."

"Can I ride back with you?"

"It depends on how things go. I hope so."

She reached up, gave me a hotter kiss and bumped me hard once with her pelvis. Then she slipped through the door, put her face in the narrow opening, whispered, "I hope you ache all night," and firmly shut me out.

Chapter 24

I was in Matt's kitchen drinking orange juice when he came in. He was breathing heavily and had a welt on his cheek where he told me he'd been struck by a branch that snapped back when he followed Handy too closely.

"Lost him," he said, flopping down in a chair. I offered him orange juice, which he accepted and drank thirstily.

"Come right down to it, we never knew what the hell we were chasing—never saw a thing, and with all our racket and Jesse's barking, we sure as hell didn't hear anything else. Jesse lost whatever it was at the county road. He's not exactly a bloodhound."

"Everybody gone to bed up at the big house?" I asked.

"Yeah. Geoffrey left as soon as we came back and said we found nothing; Jerry and Phyl, Sorah and Pam, all sacked out. Handy's still prowling with Jesse."

"Someday he's going to need sleep."

"He's a great catnapper. Don't worry about Handy."

"What would have happened if you guys caught Thorvald?"

He finished his orange juice, set the glass down and blinked at me.

"No idea. I guess I never believed we'd actually catch the bastard. Handy and I figure the chase would be enough to scare him off. My God, the sound of us blundering through the brush and Jesse's baying like a hound of hell would've scared off Satan."

The combination of a day's drinking and the mad chase through the woods had depleted his energy. He apologetically wished me good night and went to bed.

I found Handy with Jesse by Burt's cabin, and we discussed Thorvald's likeliest next move. Neither of us considered the possibility it hadn't been him they chased. He agreed with me that the isolated white house was his least likely target. Handy said he'd continue patrolling around the two west cabins if I'd keep watch on Matt's place.

I walked slowly back along the shore listening to the frog chorus which seemed comforting, probably because I remembered seeing a horror movie where when the monster appeared, all nature was silenced. A dog barked in the distance, and Jesse responded with his own, but only once.

After circling Matt's cabin and making a stop at the outhouse, I walked down to the dock. The Milky Way formed a long band of white across the black sky.

Jesse barked again, this time with urgency. I listened, trying to guess if he were moving, but couldn't tell. It occurred to me I needed a weapon, or at least a flashlight, and I started to run for the cabin while listening for the dog. His barking became more frantic, then slacked off and suddenly ceased.

I charged from the kitchen, found Matt's flashlight on a shelf and ran toward the white house. There were no lights evident, and I raced on toward Burt's cabin. As I passed Luke's place there was a whoosh and a bright flame leaped skyward from its rear.

I found the front door locked and was clutching the knob as I heard movement inside and Marcia's commanding voice. As I lifted my hand to knock, the door was jerked open and Luke appeared, silhouetted by fire. He was carrying Billy and Marcia was immediately behind him, leading Sandra.

"Get to the white house," Marcia ordered Luke. "Call for help."

He ignored her and asked me where Jesse was.

"With Handy—I heard him barking—then he stopped—"

He handed Billy to Marcia and started yelling for Handy. She tightened her mouth, told Sandra to stay close and began running clumsily toward the white house.

Burt and Peg came running with their boys, and Burt said he'd called the fire department and sheriff's office.

"We've got to catch that goddamned maniac!" he yelled.

Luke brushed him off as he had Marcia, and ran down to the beach to turn on the pump he had submerged there as a source of water for his vegetable garden, and scrambled for the hose to spray his cabin.

I abandoned them and sprinted back toward Matt's place thinking Thorvald might strike there while everyone was preoccupied with Luke's fire.

Matt met me on his path, barefooted and in shorts, waved off my concern for his place and said we'd help Luke. As we approached, we could see the entire cabin ablaze and flames already spreading into the woods. Burt and Luke were running toward the dock, and Luke stopped to tell us Handy had intercepted Thorvald trying to escape south, chased him back toward the lake and saw him shove off in Luke's rowboat. As he spoke, Burt was scrambling to untie his speedboat from the dock.

"Where's Handy?" I asked Luke.

"Up by the cabin—he sprained or broke his ankle chasing Thorvald through the woods—"

"Come on," yelled Burt.

We ran to join him and began scrambling into the boat, but he yelled no, he could carry only three. Matt was still on the dock and backed off. Before I could object or offer

157

my space, Burt had hit the starter, slammed the throttle forward. I'd have tumbled into the water if Luke hadn't grabbed my arm.

"Get the light on him," yelled Burt.

For a second, after regaining balance, I couldn't find the fugitive. Then he was in sight, his face white in the flashlight's glare, bobbing as he stroked frantically, his mouth twisted in a wild grimace.

He turned to check his bow, which was aimed at the point, now only a few dozen yards away.

Burt headed straight for him and the rowboat seemed frozen in the water. Just before certain collision, Burt laid the boat over on the gunwale, straightened us up, laid it on the other side and cut back. The rowboat bobbed wildly while Thorvald kept fighting the oars. We circled him, darted in, then cut away.

He howled.

Burt cut in sharply, killed the motor, and Luke grabbed the rowboat bow. Thorvald howled again, leaped up, dragged the right oar from its lock and raised it high. Before he could swing, Luke kicked the bow, throwing the madman to his knees. The oar splashed into the water. Luke leaped on the rowboat and closed with Thorvald who screamed, staggered erect and hurled Luke into the lake. As he turned toward us I saw him jerk the hatchet from his belt. The light from my flash showed black stains on the blade and I knew Jesse was dead.

Burt spoke to me, his voice suddenly calm.

I saw he was offering the minnow net, which was about the size of a shortened tennis net. I glanced at Thorvald who took a tentative step toward us, trying to shield his eyes against the light with his left hand while brandishing the hatchet with his right.

"What about Luke?" I yelled.

As I reached for the net, the rowboat heaved violently, there was a great splash and Thorvald was gone. It took me a second to realize Luke had gripped the gunwale from the water and jerked hard enough to spill our prey.

"Nice work," Burt told Luke as we dragged him in beside us.

"Think he can swim?" Luke gasped.

"Maybe," said Burt.

"I think he went straight down," I said.

I'd seen the water surface break behind them and wasn't about to point it out.

"He's lost his hatchet," said Luke, "he's harmless now."

"Gimme the flashlight," Burt ordered.

I handed it over.

He swept the beam over the dark water, back and forth, all around and just caught the tiny swirl as Thorvald went under a few yards between us and the point.

In the distance we heard approaching sirens.

"You should leave this to the police now," I said.

"The hell with that," said Burt. "He's been getting away for days. We'll get him now."

Luke was silent and Burt hit the starter. As soon as we were under way, he handed the light to Luke, then slammed the throttle into full speed and streaked toward where the water had swirled. Once there, he circled cautiously. I glanced back at the shore, saw Luke's place still burning and the trees blazing. Sparks tumbled against the sky. There seemed to be dozens of people scrambling like ants. I hoped they were firefighters.

As I turned back, the water bulged ten feet away to my right. Luke swung the light around and nailed Thorvald's white face, glaring eyes and streaming black hair.

Burt hit full speed, laid the boat on its side and streaked toward him. I expected a reduction in speed or another turn, but neither happened and I yelled, "You'll hit him!"

At once I felt the sickening impact, heard the motor falter and skip, then roar again. I sank back, folded my arms and closed my eyes. The afterglow of the fire on shore stayed in my mind, and I looked at the redness until it ran.

Chapter 25

Volunteer firemen were unable to save the cabin, but quickly ended the forest fire. They found a seining hose beside Burt's Winnebago and a bucket near Luke's place, which made it easy to figure why the cabin had gone up so swiftly.

While it was obvious the danger was gone, the Krueger family and guests gathered in the white house as though under siege. The four children were put to bed upstairs in one room. Peg suggested it, saying it would ease at least some of the evening's trauma for them. I could see that Marcia wasn't convinced, but she didn't argue.

No one was interested in reviving the fireplace fire and most made drinks they nursed moodily while Matt and I stood by the front windows watching boats and lights down on the lake where the search for Thorvald's body was under way.

"Where's Handy?" I asked Matt.

"Geoffrey took him to a doctor in town—see about his ankle."

"Ann Rose go along?"

"Believe it or not."

I wondered if that meant she had changed her mind and decided she wanted to marry the man after all. Then I figured it was more likely the competition for Sorah's attention, since Phyl arrived, was too annoying, and Ann Rose was happy for an excuse to get away for a while.

The silence behind us was broken as Jerry, who'd been drinking steadily, spoke to Marcia.

"Well, you finally got 'im."

I glanced around and saw Marcia scowl at her brother-in-law.

"What's that supposed to mean?"

"You managed it. Killing poor dumb Thorvald. You put Luke and Burt up to torching his place, didn't you? Figured that'd run him off and leave your precious babes safe. Only it backfired a little. He hit back. But in the end it'll go your way. The cabin was insured and you can rebuild, and everything'll be peachy again, right?"

"You're one to talk," said Marcia. "You finally got what you wanted too, didn't you?"

"Huh?"

"You brought Sorah here."

"What's that got to do with anything?"

"You knew P.J. was a fool for young women; that's what really started you back. Then you brought Sorah here, knowing he'd fall for her, and she could tie him around her little finger and take everything. You knew you'd never get a cent of his money, and you couldn't stand us getting it. So you and your lesbian girlfriend brought her in through poor dumb Matt, and the three of you did away with P.J."

"Hey, Marcia," said Luke, reaching for her arm, "come on!"

Jerry sat up and laughed as Marcia jerked away from her husband.

"Let 'er rave," he said. "She's gotta get it off her chest. Tell us more. How'd we manage it?"

"Something to do with his medication. He got something from that clinic where those two harpies nursed. It'd be easy for them to work out—"

"So that's why you brought the poor man's Sherlock here, huh?"

He turned to me. "You got it all figured out to suit her?"

"He found out that P.J. took shots," said Sorah. For the first time she looked angry. "I told him all about it when he asked."

Marcia scowled at me. "When'd she tell you that?"

"Today."

"So. Is the medicine still around?"

"No," I looked at Sorah. "We checked the medicine cabinet and it was gone."

"How about the bureau beside the bed?" asked Marcia.

Sorah's head lifted a fraction, and her eyes flickered toward me and back to Marcia.

"How'd you know he kept it there?" asked Sorah.

"I didn't—it's just that'd be the most obvious place to look . . ."

Marcia's voice was casual but the answer was too quick.

"Okay, folks," said Luke loudly, "it's time for bed. Some of us have to be back at work tomorrow—"

Matt, who had never turned his head from watching out the window, spoke over his shoulder.

"Looks like they've found Thorvald."

Everyone surged to the windows and stared down at the lake where boats were converging on the still water. After a few moments, two men in the center boat began dragging something dark up over the side. One volunteer lost his balance and nearly tumbled into the lake, but a companion jerked him erect roughly, as though offended by a note of farce in a tragic scene.

I thought I saw blood through the tattered dark clothing before it occurred to me water would rinse it away. The redness was lacerated flesh.

The boats began moving toward shore, and as the floodlights winked out, the lake surface turned tar black and the small fleet became ominous.

"I'm going down there," said Matt. "They'll need somebody to identify him."

I walked with him to the dock and halted on the sand as Matt strode with echoing steps out to the boats nudging against the dock pilings. Men lifted the limp, dripping body onto the pale planks, and I heard muttered conversation between a man in a sheriff's uniform and Matt as they stared down at what had been a man.

Seconds later Matt rejoined me and we walked slowly toward the house.

"You can't believe," he whispered hoarsely, "such a skinny guy could have so much meat . . . He looks plowed over."

A firefighter who'd been checking the perimeters of the fire met us on the path.

"Damn sorry about all this, Matt, but at least we stopped the spread. Thought you should know we found a dog up by the country road. Big collie with tags saying he belonged to a guy named MacGlothlin. One of your guests?"

"His daughter is—what about the dog?"

"Looks like somebody split his head with an axe. Deader'n hell."

Matt thanked him for the information and his work, and we went on.

Nearly everyone was standing around looking exhausted and depressed as we re-entered the living room. Matt confirmed his identification of the dead man as Thorvald. I went over to Pam and took her aside.

"Why's everybody gone ape about that maniac getting killed?" she whispered. "You'd think they'd be relieved."

"There's guilt and more," I said.

164

"What about what Marcia said—is she nuts?"

"Not quite. Listen, I've got bad news—"

"Oh God, don't tell me. Jesse's dead, isn't he?"

I nodded.

She shook her head and her eyes began to water. "The poor dumb mutt. I knew it. When he caught up with that man he more than likely wagged his tail and grinned and—oh shit!"

She pulled away from me and ran upstairs.

Matt told the crowd about Jesse's death, and I could sense at once a change in attitude as feelings hardened against Thorvald, easing the general sense of guilt over even remote involvement with the motorboat murder. I saw Burt take a deep breath, let it out and walk to make a drink.

Sorah drifted over to my side as Luke took Marcia's arm, and they went upstairs without looking back.

"Where are they going to sleep?" I asked.

"Wherever they want. Ann Rose and Handy can stay with Matt again if his leg gets fixed and they come back. What've you figured out?"

"Just about everything except what I'm going to do about it."

"Tell me."

I glanced at Matt and saw him helping Phyl get Jerry to his feet. Jerry was playing the drunk full tilt, rubbery and giggling.

"Ol' Marcia's put a hex on me," he told his assistants, "took the bones outta my legs. I'll be awright, just need a nap."

They got him between them and half-carried him up the long stairway.

"Let's take a walk," I said to Sorah.

We went outside. It was late enough so mosquitoes were

no bother, and we strolled to the dock, sat down and dangled our legs over the water. A gentle breeze blew in from the northeast and rippled the lake surface just enough to lap audibly on the beach.

"The way I see it," I told her, "Marcia planned to frame you for murder. I don't think she was ever in love with the old man, but she's got a thing for power that's stronger than greed, and she let him make love to her thinking it'd keep her in control, only of course it didn't work. You came along and, in her eyes, turned him all the way against her and topped it off by getting yourself made the sole heir. So she decided to kill him and pin it on you. That'd take care of her jealousy in the first place, and get rid of you so her family'd inherit in the second place. Marcia figured it'd seem obvious to anybody that you'd be the natural suspect. You'd been a nurse, you had Phyl as a close friend still working in a clinic. She might even have considered blackmailing you into turning over money to her if she thought she had a good enough case, but couldn't get a formal prosecution going. And finally, I think, she convinced herself you'd have a record of promiscuity, maybe a solid lesbian background that'd make you vulnerable if she got me to do an investigation of your past."

I felt movement on the dock behind us and suffered a shock of *deja vu* before turning, in full expectation of seeing Thorvald's ghost, but it was only Peg. She came on, wearing a long robe and thongs.

"I can't stand it," she said. "I've got to know what's going on. What was that business between Marcia and Jerry? How'd Marcia know what happened between Jerry and Dad?"

"I'd guess Luke told her," I said. "It was Estelle, wasn't it? Jerry opened a door he shouldn't have and saw them."

Peg sank down on the dock and hugged her knees.

"It absolutely ruined Jerry. It ruined everything. And it's made everybody horrible. Did Daddy betray you too, Sorah? Is that why you killed him?"

"I didn't do it, Peg. Believe me. That's all Marcia's idea. And your father never betrayed me; I guarantee you that. He didn't want to and probably couldn't if he'd tried. He could only make love after getting his shot, and I gave it to him, not knowing the medicine had been changed."

Chapter 26

"I'm sorry I lied to you before," Sorah said with little noticeable remorse, "but Marcia was trying to have you prove I killed P.J., and that made me leery of admitting I gave him that last shot. He wasn't squeamish about anything else I know of, but he hated the needle and couldn't stand poking it into himself."

I suspected he got a sneaky kick from his ladylove hurting him at the beginning of the sex act, but kept my dirty-old-man thoughts quiet.

"Did he ever tell you why Jerry ran away?" I asked.

"No. I didn't know anything about what happened back then until the talk between Marcia and Jerry tonight. Jerry never said a word of it and certainly P.J. didn't. It always seemed strange because I was briefed on everyone else, as if joining the family were some kind of CIA operation." She smiled at Peg. "He told me, 'Just be yourself with Peg and she'll love you. Don't even try to reach Marcia. She's a consummate hater. Avoid her when you can, don't let her make you mad, ignore her digs. She's smart enough to see she'd only make herself look bad if she attacks and you don't respond. Force her to be civil by always being a perfect lady.' "

"What'd he say about Matt?" asked Peg. "How were you supposed to handle him?"

I felt she took too long for her answer to be altogether frank.

"Matt was very special to P.J.," she said slowly. "He never felt he understood him but had great respect. He said

I could depend on him to be a gentleman, but it would be kindest if I did absolutely nothing to encourage him."

"I don't think 'respect' quite fits," said Peg with a rare edge on her voice. "He was more likely to think of gentlemen as pretty ridiculous. Did you tell him what Matt said about P.J. when he found out his father was the one you were after?"

Sorah didn't appreciate the way that was put but managed a gentle smile.

"No, not a word."

"Did he ask?"

She said no. I wasn't sure Peg believed her, but she didn't pursue the subject.

"What did he say about Burt?" I asked.

Sorah frowned and shrugged. "About what you'd expect, I imagine. He said don't trust him, be cool, let him think you're charitably inclined and, for Peg's benefit, don't let him know when you think he's an ass."

Peg smiled and nodded. "That sounds just like him."

We were silent a moment, and then Peg wriggled to the dock edge beside Sorah and dangled her legs over with ours.

"I've got to ask," she said. "Did P.J. die making love?"

"No. He didn't have a chance. The shot didn't revive him, it killed him."

"So it was murder, but not by you. Then who?"

"Ask Kyle."

Peg looked at me.

I suggested we go over to Matt's place and talk the whole thing over.

"You know who did it?" Peg demanded.

"I'll tell you at Matt's cabin. All the family should be in on it, but I'll settle for those still up."

We found Matt and Jerry sitting before the dead fire-place drinking coffee. Phyl had gone to bed. Like a few drunks I've known, Jerry had almost miraculous recuperative powers. His eyes were relatively clear now and his speech was almost normal.

"I can tell from the P.I.'s eye, he's cracked the case," said Jerry. "Now he gathers all the suspects and is gonna spring the final solution, right?"

"Shut up, Jerry," said Peg, "this isn't a comedy."

Matt offered coffee, we all took some and sat crowded around his little table as I began.

"I think P.J. was murdered, and believe I know who did it. And no, I'm not going through any Nero Wolfe scene. You people have a problem, it's not mine. You have to decide how to settle it."

"Murder's every man's problem," said Jerry, "and no man's an island—"

Matt, Peg and Sorah stared him into silence and then looked at me.

"One person had the motive, the means and the opportunity to kill him. You all know P.J. was impotent, that he went to the clinic and got a prescription to remedy it. Maybe you don't all know he took shots immediately before making love so he could get an erection, but Sorah gave me the story. And the last time he took the shot it was lethal. I believe insulin was substituted for the papaverine hydrochloride. It's colorless and hard to detect. Since he was nearly sixty-five years old, it was natural for the doctor who was called in to assume it was heart failure. With the body turned over to the University for research, it wasn't likely anyone would be examining it in a way to identify anything exceptional. Certainly not in any hurry."

"You're saying it was Marcia," said Jerry, sitting forward. "She'd have insulin handy; she could've done the job when she went to the bathroom while the family was playing poker earlier that night—"

"I don't believe it," said Peg. "That's monstrous. Is that what you're saying, Kyle?"

"I'm saying it seems likely."

"But why?" she cried. "What'd she gain by killing him? Sorah was his only heir—"

"And if Sorah got the blame, the family would collect."

"My God, but think of her kids, and mine, Luke, all of us—"

"It's all guesswork," said Matt. "You can't ruin a whole family because of some cockeyed theory."

"Come on," yelled Jerry, "this is a cold-blooded, selfish bitch. She killed P.J. just like she killed that nut Thorvald, because she did, you know. She manipulated that whole disgusting mess. Did you see her face when I accused her? And how she tried to turn things around and put P.J.'s murder on Sorah, Phyl, and me? You going to let her get away with that?"

"All right," said Matt, putting his hand on Jerry's forearm. "Let's calm down." He looked at me. "Tell us what you think happened. We'll hear you out."

"Fine, I'd appreciate that. You all know Marcia has diabetes and takes insulin daily. Right?"

They nodded.

"Jerry learned about the shots from Phyl, and it was something too sweet to keep to himself."

He admitted that.

"The last time P.J. took his shot, he died. I believe that night, when everyone was playing poker, Marcia took a break, went up to the master bedroom with her purse. She took out her insulin and syringe, found P.J.'s medication in

171

the bureau beside his bed. She removed papaverine from
P.J.'s bottle with her syringe, and refilled it with her insulin.
Then she returned to the poker game. I suspect she even
guessed that Sorah gave the shot to P.J., so her fingerprints
would be on the syringe if the examining doctor decided it
was something he should check out."

"I don't get it," said Matt. "Why can Marcia take insulin
safely while P.J. couldn't?"

I turned to Sorah.

"Because," she said, "diabetics take carefully measured
amounts to meet their special problem and the dosage is
small. P.J. was used to taking four cc's of papaverine. That
much insulin was as deadly as a forty-five slug."

They stared at her in silence.

"So now," I said, "it's up to you. If you say nothing,
nothing more'll come of all this. Maybe. Peg's mostly concerned about what prosecution in a family murder will do to
the survivors. I understand that. But you've got to face the
risk that your sister-in-law murdered your father, and tried
to frame Sorah for it. Maybe she won't try to murder
anyone else and'll be a good mother and a more faithful
wife. But, as Jerry pointed out, she's manipulative, cold-
blooded, and single-minded. She wanted to hire me to in-
vestigate Sorah because, hating her as she did, she was posi-
tive I'd dig up something really bad about her and would
believe she was evil enough to kill P.J. I don't believe she'll
give up because it didn't work out. She's damned intelligent, totally unscrupulous and wants power."

"Hell yes," agreed Jerry. "If she managed to pin the
murder on Sorah and got quarter share of the family loot,
she'd probably start chopping down the rest of us."

"Oh," said Peg in disgust, "don't be an idiot."

Matt turned to Sorah.

172

"What do you think? You believe she won't give up?"

She shook her head. "I can't grasp all of this; it's too awful. Let's not think about it any more now. We should get some sleep and think soberly."

"It's up to you people," I said. "If you think your father's murder calls for revenge, justice or whatever, you have to blow the whistle, not me."

I turned to Sorah and asked what room Pam was sleeping in at her house.

She gave me a startled look, started to ask a question, thought better of it and said, "First one, top of the stairs."

I thanked her, went to my room, packed my stuff and walked out. Sorah looked at me as I passed through, then turned back to face Matt who was talking very quietly.

I found Pam reading in bed at the big house and told her I was going back to Minneapolis. If she wanted to go along she'd have to hustle.

She batted her eyes, said okay and got up. I waited below and surprisingly soon she came down lugging her suitcase. I took it, carried it to my car and as I slammed the trunk lid, Matt appeared.

"You don't have to go, do you?" he asked plaintively.

"Yeah, I do."

"Well, thanks, I guess."

"Don't mention it. I'll see you."

As we drove out Pam asked if I wanted to talk about what had happened and I said no. She said okay and after a while went to sleep. When we got to her house, I carried her bag to the door, and she apologized for sleeping all the way.

"Aren't you going to tell me what happened at the lake?" she asked.

"Maybe one day. Not now."

When I kissed her goodbye she squeezed me hard but didn't offer a pelvic bump.

"Give me a call," she said.

"Sure."

Chapter 27

The first days after the Fourth I kept expecting to hear from Matt or Peg. It even seemed possible I'd hear directly from the police or find an article in the newspaper about an investigation of P.J.'s death. None of these things happened.

In September there was an article about the divorce of Margaret (Peg) Beattie, daughter of the recently deceased millionaire, P.J. Krueger. It covered three columns, with two short paragraphs reporting that Peg was awarded custody of her two children, and all of the rest outlined her colorful father's great business career.

A week later the paper carried an announcement of the wedding of Margaret (Peg) Krueger and Gregory Talbott.

Geoffrey Ashland called the afternoon that appeared, identified himself modestly, as though anyone meeting him would be likely to forget, and asked if by any chance I had Sorah's current address. I said I only knew the one at the lake.

"She left there. The place is up for sale."

I said that was news to me.

"I take it you haven't been in touch with the family since the Fourth?"

I admitted that was so.

There was a long silence and finally he sighed and asked, "What happened after I left that night? There was a family blowup, wasn't there? Was it because P.J. left everything to Sorah, or was it something to do with how he died?"

"What makes you think there was a blowup?"

"When I found her number disconnected, I called Luke

and asked what happened to Sorah. He said she'd moved somewhere, wasn't sure where. Gave me some business about her traveling a while, trying to decide what to do with herself. It sounded like there'd been a complete cut-off. I called Matt, but he's gone back to California, and I got no answer to the number Luke gave me."

"Try Jerry."

"I did. His number's disconnected too."

"What about Peg?"

"She's off to Barbados on a honeymoon. Didn't even invite me to her wedding."

"Well, it's possible Phyl knows where Sorah is. They were roommates once."

"Phyl? Wasn't she Jerry's girlfriend?"

"That's right."

"What's her last name?"

"I don't know."

There was another long silence.

"All right, what about that Ann Rose?"

I didn't know her last name either, but said I'd give Handy a call and see if he was in touch. Geoffrey said that'd be appreciated and put it in a dollar sign tone.

I looked in the phone book and found thirty-five H. Andersons listed. That made me think a while and finally I took a whack at checking sports supply companies, and found him with the third try. He told me Ann Rose was somewhere with Sorah. He had no idea where, and I got the impression he had been able to get over her.

Finally I called Geoffrey at his office and wound up with a call-back in the evening. I told him what I'd heard from Handy.

"I see," he said.

"You want me to follow up?"

"No," he said quietly, and hung up.

It didn't surprise me that I never got a check from him.

The last I heard about the family appeared in the obituary section of the *Minneapolis Star Tribune.* It reported that Marcia Krueger, wife of Luke Krueger and daughter-in-law of the recently deceased millionaire, P.J. Krueger, had died of an apparent overdose of insulin.

About the Author

Harold Adams has spent most of his life in the Midwest, where he has observed the lives of his friends and neighbors. After graduating with a degree in English from the University of Minnesota and serving in the U.S. Army, he worked for several years with the Minneapolis Better Business Bureau.

His Carl Wilcox series played a vital role in reviving the historical mystery, with his accurate recreation of a Depression-era small town standing as one of the major achievements in contemporary mystery fiction.

Now Harold returns with his other series character, Kyle Champion, whom he first introduced in *When Rich Men Die*. No matter whom he's writing about, Harold brings the same skills, compassion and sly wit to each adventure.

The employees of Five Star hope you have enjoyed this book. All our books are made to last. Other Five Star books are available at your library, through selected bookstores, or directly from us.

For information about titles, please call:

(800) 223-1244

or visit our Web site at:

www.gale.com/fivestar

To share your comments, please write:

Publisher
Five Star
295 Kennedy Memorial Drive
Waterville, ME   04901